The Rules of *Never*

The Rules of *Never*

A Middle School Survival Guide

by

Phil Adam

This book is a work of fiction. Names, characters, places and incidents are the product of the author's imagination or are used fictitiously. Any resemblance to actual events, locales or persons, living or dead, is entirely coincidental.

ISBN 978-1537395678

To My Former Students

Acknowledgements

I wish to thank the following individuals who were helpful in the production of this book: Matt Imig, Dale DeVillers, Lin Persick, Craig VanSlyke, Greg Sauve, Jane Ryder, Karen Loos, Kim Dziatkewich, Den Persick and Mary Capo for their input; Chris Larson and Joe Layden for their suggestions; Carolyn Paplham for illustrations and cover design; draft readers: Bill Gilbert, Nancy Kohrman, Brenda Bryfczynski, Lynne Turkus, Donna Jahnke and Audra Turkus; professional editors: Karinya Funsett-Topping, Shannon Roberts and Doug Wagner; Steve Frozena and Bill Wheeler for their assistance in editing and proofreading and Den Persick for his help in layout, design and publishing. And finally, my wife, Ellen for her continuing support and encouragement.

CONTENTS

PROLOGUE

My first day at Lost Creek Middle School was to begin in less than nine hours. I lay in bed wide awake with worry, a hundred concerns racing through my mind.

What if I lost my assignment, forgot my hall pass or misplaced my books?

Surely, the rules I'd learned at orientation would get me through the year. After all, Lost Creek has rules for *everything*: how to dress, how not to dress, being tardy, being absent, leaving school early, leaving school late, lunchroom conduct, hallway conduct, classroom conduct. Not to mention the no-nos plastered everywhere: no running, no talking, no gum, no phones, no shoving, no bullying, no name-calling. It looked like Lost Creek had thought of every rule possible.

Or had they?

I sat up, beads of sweat forming on my forehead. I switched on the lamp on my nightstand, bounded out of bed and grabbed a notebook and a purple marker lying on my desk. I scrawled *THE RULES OF NEVER* on the cover in case Lost Creek had forgotten any. I tucked the notebook into the drawer and wiped my forehead with my pajama sleeve.

Relieved, I crawled back under the covers and turned off the lamp.

RULE ONE

NEVER SKIP THE FIRST DAY OF MIDDLE SCHOOL

I like daisies but not when someone tries cramming one up my nose.

My troubles began after I parked my rusty, battered Schwinn in the last slot of the school's bike rack. As I unwrapped my lock, Caden Jacobs rammed his BMX's front tire into my rear wheel.

I whipped around and glared at him. "What'd you do that for?"

"You're in my spot, man. It's reserved for me." Caden backed up his bike.

Was he gonna ram mine again?

Caden had been in my third grade class at Valley Crest Elementary, but I moved near the end of the school year. I hadn't seen him since, and he sure had changed. He was as big as an ox, tall for a sixth grader and outweighed me by a good forty pounds. His long legs seemed out of proportion to his upper body, but his most noticeable feature was his Adam's apple. It stuck out as if a chicken wing were caught in his throat.

"You can't reserve spaces in a bike rack," I said.

"Can so. Ask the guy over there." Caden pointed to a short potbellied man standing by the flagpole.

I pulled my cable lock through my front wheel.

"Move that piece of junk." Caden hopped off the BMX. "Now!"

I locked my bike to the rack. I wasn't worried about Caden. I'd dealt with kids at my old school who thought they owned the place.

After propping his bike against the end of the rack, Caden marched over and shoved me.

I whirled around, trying to appear threatening. "You're asking for it."

Caden pounded his fist into his palm. "Am I supposed to be afraid?" He shoved me again, this time harder. I lost my balance and fell against my bike, smacking my knee on the pedal.

That hurt.

I stepped toward Caden, clenched my fist and slugged him in the gut. He doubled over and sank to his knees. "Warned ya."

He glared up at me, his eyes ablaze. "You're gonna pay for that, Abrams." He spit, missing my sneaker by inches.

Wanting to start middle school on the right foot, I walked away.

"Did ya hear me?" Caden yelled.

I kept walking.

Caden ran up behind me and pushed me so hard I stumbled. When I regained my footing, I spun around and faced him. He stood like a boxer, with fists raised and a crazed look in his eyes. Without warning, he threw a left at my head.

I ducked in time but didn't see his right, which nailed me in the shoulder. My knees wobbled, but I kept my balance.

Figuring my only chance of surviving was to wrestle him, I kicked him in the shin. Then, while he clutched his leg and hopped on one foot, I rushed him, knocking him to the ground. Seconds later, we were rolling around in a bed of daisies.

"Fight! Fight!" hollered a boy standing nearby. Kids hurried over and crowded around us.

The scuffle ended when a brawny man I assumed was a teacher burst through the ring of spectators.

"Knock it off!" He seized each of us by the wrist with his muscular hands and pulled us apart.

We stopped wrestling and scrambled to our feet. Caden rubbed a golf ball-size knob on his shin, while I massaged my shoulder and licked a small cut on my lower lip.

"You two come with me."

"Can I lock my bike?" Caden asked.

"Forget it. Now get moving."

"If my bike is stolen, it's your fault."

The teacher gave Caden a stern look and led us into the school's main entrance and across a black mat as wide as the hallway. Stamped in jumbo block letters was *LOST CREEK MIDDLE SCHOOL*. Below the lettering was an imprint of a frog, the school's mascot.

A short distance from the entrance, a huge orange and black ceiling banner read "WELCOME FROGS." *My first day of sixth grade and I'm already wearing out my welcome.*

"Abrams started it," Caden told the teacher as we marched down the freshly waxed locker-lined hallway that smelled like Mr. Clean. "He parked his bike in my spot."

"You can't reserve parking spots, can you?" I asked the teacher.

"Talk to the principal," he said with such authority that I was afraid to say anything more.

I started to worry. Was Caden right?

"Is the assistant principal in?" the teacher asked after we walked into the office.

A woman stood at her desk rearranging a mountain of papers. Tall to begin with, she wore a bright yellow outfit and sported a big fluffy hairdo that made her appear even taller, like Big Bird.

When we stepped up to the counter, she stopped sorting papers. "Mr. Mullen just wrapped up his meeting with the music teachers." Her phone rang and she reached to pick it up. "Should be here any minute."

The teacher went over to the recycle bin and came back with a folded sheet of paper. "Need your names." He eyeballed Caden. "You are?"

"Caden Jacobs."

The teacher snatched a pen from the counter and scribbled Caden's name on the scrap paper. Then he looked at me. "And your name?"

"Phil Abrams."

He jotted down my name and wrote something else.

"Please give this message to Mr. Mullen," he said to the secretary, setting the note on the counter.

Still on the phone, Big Bird mouthed, "Okay."

After hesitating for a moment, the teacher turned to us. "Take a seat." He pointed at a bright orange bench with black legs.

Caden and I sat down next to each other.

"At opposite ends," the teacher directed, and we moved to our assigned spots. "You're not to talk," he added loud enough for Big Bird to hear as he rushed out the door.

I stared at the lime-colored wallpaper and chewed my nails, a nervous habit I'd picked up in first grade. The wallpaper was adorned with hundreds of short, random blue lines. To pass the time, I imagined the lines formed a maze.

Focusing my eyes, I started near the floor and worked my way toward the ceiling. I was midway up the wall when Caden noticed my green and gold sneakers.

"Green Bay Packers colors," he said in an almost pleasant way.

"My favorite football team," I said, surprised and a little suspicious that he was talking to me.

"I watch every game."

"I'm a Cheesehead, too. My cousin played wide receiver for the Chicago Bears."

"Wish I were that good. I can't even catch a cold."

Caden let out a short laugh.

Big Bird stopped plunking away at her computer and ambled up to the counter with a stern expression and her jaw jutting out.

"Aren't you two supposed to keep quiet?"

"Sorry," Caden said, sounding as if he meant it.

"Going to be a long year," she muttered under her breath as she walked back to her desk.

No longer in her line of sight, I said barely above a whisper, "Doesn't she remind you of Big Bird?"

Caden snickered. "Yeah, but she acts like Oscar the Grouch," he said in a hushed voice.

I slapped my hand over my mouth to stifle a chuckle.

For the next five minutes, we whispered like secret agents and found we had a lot in common. We had Mr. Patterson for homeroom and had the same class schedule, and we both had a younger sister. We shared a dislike for English, broccoli and going to church on Sunday, but we both enjoyed four-wheeling, video games and sci-fi movies.

As we discussed our favorite Packers, a middle-aged man sporting a closely clipped haircut hurried into the office. He had a thick neck and a slightly off-center nose, and stubble covered much of his leathery face. He wore a short-sleeve plaid shirt and black pants held up by wide brown suspenders. A crest was tattooed on his right arm. He strode up to the counter.

"Who's the lumberjack?" I asked Caden.

"Mr. Mullen, assistant principal. He's an ex-Army Ranger."

As I chomped down on my thumbnail, a chill crept all the way up my spine.

"Anything come up while I was gone?" Mr. Mullen asked Big Bird in a raspy voice. He sounded as if he'd smoked for years.

"Mr. O'Neill left a note on the counter for you."

After reading the message, the assistant principal slid the note into his shirt pocket and walked over to us, glowering.

"Already? The school year hasn't even officially begun." He shook his head. "In my office," he ordered in a voice that military men seem to master so well.

I shuddered.

The first bell rang as I rose from the bench. The horde of kids milling around outside poured into school as if they were heading into Disney World, but this time no one was smiling.

Mr. Mullen steered Caden and me down a narrow corridor to his office. He opened the door and ushered us into a carpeted room the size of a postage stamp and pulled the door shut behind him.

"Sit." He gestured to three plastic chairs parked in front of an L-shaped desk. After plunking myself down, I noticed the bronze nameplate on the desk: "MR. MULLEN, ASSISTENT PRINCIPAL." I smiled. Did Mr. Mullen know ASSISTANT was misspelled?

Mr. Mullen plopped down in his black-leather swivel armchair and pulled himself to his desk. After shuffling a pile of papers, he clasped his hands and rested his elbows on the desk. He leaned forward and studied us.

As I wiped my clammy palms on my khaki shorts and drummed my foot on the carpet, I glanced at Caden. He remained calm, as if sitting in the office were second nature to him.

"Which of you is Jacobs?" Mr. Mullen asked.

"I am," answered Caden.

Mr. Mullen shifted his attention to me. My butt got hot, and I fidgeted in my chair as if I were sitting on a mound of fire ants. I needed to chill out before my boxers caught fire.

"Sit still," Mr. Mullen barked. He cleared his

throat as if a gob of mucus were stuck in it.

Too afraid to move, I sat like a car with a dead battery.

As Mr. Mullen mangled a paper clip, he gave me the once-over. "Are you related to Kaylee Abrams, the remarkable artist I met at summer school?"

"She's, um, she's my sister," I stammered.

Mr. Mullen surprised me with a tiny smile. "I thought so," he said in a friendly tone. "You look very much alike."

Remarkable? Resemble my obnoxious nine-year-old sister? Is he kidding? But maybe this was a point in my favor. I relaxed.

Then he slammed his palm on his desk.

I almost fell off the chair. I chewed on what remained of my thumbnail and hoped the wetness in my boxers was just sweat.

Mr. Mullen took off his rimless glasses, slowly folded them and tucked them in his shirt pocket. He pushed himself away from his desk and stood. "Fighting at Lost Creek will not be tolerated," he told us in a booming voice. "Since it's your first day of school, I won't call your parents, but today and tomorrow you will report to after-school detention in Room 206."

I needed to make something positive happen on what so far was a pretty lousy day.

"But Mr. Mullen," I said, my voice quivering, "that's not fair."

"And why not, Abrams?"

"'Cause the fight was my fault. I goaded Caden into it. He shouldn't get in trouble for a fight I started."

Caden's mouth hung open. I was surprised myself.

"Is that the way it happened, Jacobs?" Mr. Mullen asked in a harsh tone.

Caden politely nodded.

Mr. Mullen's piercing bloodshot eyes shot right through me. "You're not a troublemaker, are you, Abrams? 'Cause I have no use for those kind of kids."

The question caught me off guard. Although I was no angel in school, teachers never called me a troublemaker. The only trouble I'd ever gotten into at Valley Crest happened by accident: I plugged up a toilet in kindergarten. Too afraid to tell anyone, I fled as water overflowed onto the tile floor. The bathroom flooded and water seeped

into the hallway before someone notified the office.

Later, the principal grilled me about it. After admitting I was the culprit, she gave me a one-day suspension for not reporting the problem, something that still bugs me. I bet it was the first time in Valley Crest history that a kid got suspended for pooping too much.

I thought back to that flooded bathroom. I hadn't meant to do it, of course, but I probably have a "record" because I panicked and ran. That doesn't make me a troublemaker, though. I've seen my share of troublemakers, and I'm not one of *them*, so I said, "No, sir." I hoped Mr. Mullen, being an ex-Ranger, would appreciate me calling him "sir."

Not even a faint smile crossed his lips.

"Good to hear, Abrams." He sat back down. "Your confession does change things." He leaned back in his chair. "Jacobs, I'm letting you off with a warning. Abrams, I'm adding a third night of detention. You will both have a letter placed in your file concerning this incident. Understood, boys?"

"Understood," we said at the same time.

"I trust that both of you can find your locker and your first class?"

"I think so," I said, hoping to remember them from last week's orientation session.

"Good." Mr. Mullen put on his glasses and

wrote out two admittance slips to English and one detention slip. "I don't want to see either of you in my office again." He handed us the slips. "Now get to class." He picked up a cell phone lying on his desk and began punching in numbers with his right thumb.

"Mr. Mullen, can I lock my bike?" Caden asked.

The assistant principal stopped what he was doing and peered at Caden over his glasses. "Yes, but be quick about it."

We left Mullen's office, locked Caden's bike to the rack and headed back into school. Except for two girls leaning against a wall yakking, the hallways were deserted.

"Why'd ya take the blame?" Caden asked as we approached our lockers.

"No reason for both of us to stay after," I said. "Besides, it's only three days."

"Thanks, man. I owe you one."

"No need."

"Hey, that's what pals do." Caden stopped and held out his fist for me to bump. "My friends call me C.J."

We picked up our English materials, made a pit stop at the bathroom and headed to first hour. "You throw a good punch for a runt," C.J. said as we walked down a hallway lined with colorful motivational posters.

"I'm bigger than you think." I threw my shoulders back to look taller.

"Oh, yeah." C.J. stooped to tie his sneaker. "How big are ya?"

"Four-ten, seventy-nine pounds."

"Man, I was that big in fourth grade." C.J. laughed.

I laughed, too.

As I biked home after detention, I rode past two guys playing catch. For some reason, it reminded me of what my Little League coach told the team after winning our first game: "Boys, life is made of moments and memories." I don't remember much about the game, but I'll never forget his comment.

And I won't ever forget my first day at Lost Creek. I began the day wrestling in a flowerbed and ended it in detention. In between, I made a friend.

That's reason enough to never skip the first day of middle school.

RULE TWO

NEVER PULL DOWN YOUR PANTS WITH THE DOOR UNLOCKED

I gazed out the smudged school bus window and watched C.J. sprint down the cracked sidewalk. Just another ho-hum Friday.

Spotting C.J., the bus driver waited and pushed the handle to open the door. The door folded open and C.J. climbed aboard. I waved and caught his eye. Panting, he hustled down the aisle, slipped off his stuffed backpack and slid into the seat beside me. When he took off his New York Yankees baseball cap, I couldn't believe what I saw.

"*What happened to your hair?*" I said.

"Got tired of combing it," he said before putting his cap back over his buzz cut. "Mom cut it last night."

"You look like a dimpled chimp."

"Still better-looking than you."

"You kidding? With *those* ears?"

"Whatever." C.J. reached into his backpack, dug out his English book and dumped the book bag onto the floor.

"Why ya getting your book out?" I asked.

"Reviewing for the parts-of-speech test." He leafed through the textbook until he found the page he wanted. The black bold-faced heading on the page read "**VERBS**."

"*What test?* Joyner never mentioned a test."

"Told us yesterday. You must've been counting dead flies in the ceiling lights again."

"Real funny," I said. "What am I gonna do? I didn't study."

"Wing it, I guess." C.J. buried his nose in his book.

After art, English was my worst subject. I hated them both but for different reasons. As far as art, I didn't have an ounce of talent: my watercolors ran, my clay sculptures sagged and my self-portraits looked like zombies. Even drawing stick figures was a challenge.

To understand why I hated English, ask anyone who knows Ms. Joyner. She had a heart of stone and no patience, and her lack of passion for teaching was infectious. Yawning was a way of life in her class. We weren't itching to learn, we were itching to leave. I'd struggled with English for years, but add a teacher with less charm than a great white shark has and, well, that made class unbearable.

Besides being unpleasant, Ms. Joyner had a keen sense of hearing. I found that out the hard way. One time, from forty feet down the hallway, her bat-like ears overheard me tell C.J., "If I graded Joyner, I'd give her an F for sense of humor."

Take last Friday when she played her favorite game, "Stump the Class."

After taking attendance, she stood and faced the class. With her right arm, she pulled an imaginary whistle twice while she held an open textbook in her left hand. "Choo-choo," she announced. "Let's take a ride on 'the learning train.' "

She studied a page in the textbook and laid the book facedown on her desk. "Can anyone define *preposition* for me?" She scanned the room hoping for an answer.

Nobody uttered a word.

Ms. Joyner narrowed her made-up eyes—never a good sign for me. She blinked twice, removed her cat-eye glasses and dabbed her left eye with a tissue.

Her vision restored, Ms. Joyner put her specs back on. She paced across the room, a fancy earring swinging beneath each ear, and stopped at my desk.

"Phil, you always have something clever to say. Can you answer the question?" she asked with a sharp edge to her voice.

"I have no idea, Ms. Joyner." I lowered my head to avoid her menacing stare and clasped my hands in my lap. As she walked away, I silently prayed that the learning train would run her over.

"Anyone want to guess?" As Ms. Joyner's eyes swept the room for a raised hand, she rubbed the back of her neck like she was getting a nasty headache. "Someone say something," she said in an irritated voice.

Her question bounced around my brain like a steel ball in a pinball machine. I didn't know the definition of *preposition*, but I knew what *proposition* meant. Both words had eleven letters and began with the letter *p*, and they sounded alike. Ms. Joyner wanted an answer, so I'd give her one. I waved my hand as if I were hailing a taxi.

"Okay, Phil, define *preposition* for the class."

"I don't know the definition, Ms. Joyner. Can I give an example instead?"

"It's *may*, not *can*." She gave me her "how dumb are you?" look.

"May I give you an example?"

"An example will be fine."

"It's when C.J. offers a girl ten dollars to dance with him."

Everyone in the room, except Ms. Joyner, laughed. Even C.J. chuckled.

"Just once, Phil, could you be serious?" she said with a scowl.

Ms. Joyner went on with the lesson. "A preposition is a word that shows the relationship between a noun or pronoun and other words in a sentence." She walked to the dry erase board and wrote, "Sam ran into the woods."

He probably had to take a leak. I copied the sentence in my notebook and yawned.

Ms. Joyner underlined *into the woods*. "*Into the woods* is called a prepositional phrase. *Into* is the preposition and *woods* is the object of the preposition. I hope this clears up any confusion."

Clear as mud.

The torture continued. She yammered on about prepositions, peppering us with examples. Alex ran *across* the road, Matt left *without* his coat and Ian lived *on* the hill. Girls got involved, too. Hanna hid *behind* the sofa, Mia rode *to* school and Ella swam *in* the lake.

By the time Ms. Joyner had written the last example on the board, my head was spinning. I left English more confused than ever.

The bus screeched to a stop in the school parking lot, and I was jolted back to reality. I had a grammar test today and had as much chance of passing the exam as I did of playing quarterback for the Packers. I needed to act fast.

I glanced at C.J. “I’m skippin’ English.”

“You *are*? How ya gonna get away with that?”

Kids in the front seats surged toward the door.

“Follow my lead,” I said as we inched our way down the aisle.

As I stepped off the bus, I pretended to slip on the last step. “Holy moly,” I shouted as my legs shot out from under me. With my arms flailing in the air, I landed hard on the coarse blacktop, my butt taking the brunt of the fall.

C.J. rushed to my side, acting concerned. “You

okay, Phil?"

I sat up and gripped my lower back with both hands. "Hurt my back."

"Here, let me help you up," C.J. said, playing along.

I reached out and grabbed his outstretched hand. As I stood, a stinging sensation pierced my butt.

Mr. Grancorbitz, a teacher on bus duty, raced over. "You all right?"

"Wrenched my back," I said, sniffling.

"You did a number on your pants, too."

"Whaddya mean?"

"You ripped a hole in the seat."

"Great." I ran my hand across my rear. "These are my favorite jeans."

"Let's worry about your pants later and get you into school." He turned to C.J. "Grab an arm."

With C.J. holding one arm and Mr. G the other, we slowly made our way into the school and down the long brightly lighted hallway. About halfway, we stopped next to a display case filled with student artwork.

Mr. G let go of my arm. "Might want to have the nurse check you out."

"Probably should." I twisted my head so Mr. G didn't notice the grin on my face. His suggestion made missing English foolproof.

"Do you need help getting there?" he asked.

"No, thanks." I shook my head. "If I do, C.J. will help me."

"Well, have to get back to bus duty," Mr. G said. "Hope you're okay. Don't forget to see the nurse."

"I won't."

After he left, C.J. said, "Great acting job, Phil."

"You know what? My back and my butt do hurt. I fell harder than I meant to."

"At least you won't have to worry about fooling the nurse."

"For sure." I leaned against a locker for support. "Tell Ms. Joyner I went to the health room."

"I'll tell her you're deathly ill."

"Don't cheer her up too much."

C.J. chuckled. "See you in social studies." He headed outside to wait for the bell.

I shuffled my way to see the nurse with a hand pressed against my back and a pained expression on my face. I approached the health room not knowing what to expect.

Outside the room stood a short, stocky woman with gray hair, rosy cheeks and thick, bushy eyebrows that met in the middle. She smelled like cinnamon. The plastic name tag pinned to her shirt read "NURSE JOHNSON."

"Nurse Johnson, I'm Phil Abrams." I nervously

stuck out my hand.

"Pleased to meet you, Phil." The nurse firmly shook my hand. "How may I help you?" Her soft voice and friendly smile put me at ease.

"Hurt my back." I placed my hand on my lower back to show her where the pain was. "Mr. Grancorbitz said I should see you."

"Why don't we go into the health room?"

The nurse led me into a mustard-colored room not much bigger than a walk-in closet. Lemon-scented disinfectant hung in the air. On one side of the room was a metal-frame bed. On the other side, a tiny sink, a counter and a cabinet packed with medical supplies. Three wood-framed health posters hung on the back wall like art pieces.

"Now tell me, Phil, how you injured yourself."

"I slipped on the steps getting off the bus."

"You poor boy." The bell shrieked, signaling the start of school.

"I'll call the office and let them know you're here." The nurse reached for the phone on the counter. "What's your last name again, Phil?"

"Abrams."

The nurse punched the number for the office into the phone.

"Now let's have a look," she said after hanging up.

I turned so my backside faced the nurse.

"Your jeans have a good-size tear," she said. "I need to find out if you cut yourself." She plucked a pair of rubber gloves from a box on the counter and slipped them on. "Lower your pants."

I reluctantly dropped my jeans and boxers two-thirds of the way down my butt. "Is it bad?"

"It's red, that's all," Nurse Johnson said as she examined me. "Like a bad floor burn."

Just then the door swung open, and I twisted my head around to see a teacher barge in. Close behind him was McKenzie Harper—the last person in the world I wanted to see. Known as "Loose Lips," the sixth-grade blabbermouth kept secrets for less time than it takes to open a can of soda.

"Sorry for barging in," the teacher told Nurse Johnson. "The door was unlocked. McKenzie cut her finger. I need a dab of ointment and a bandage."

Loose Lips removed the thick-lensed glasses resting on her pimply nose and gawked at my bare butt. She plucked her phone from her backpack, but before she could take a picture, I pulled up my pants.

The teacher shooed Loose Lips from the room and got what he'd come for from the cabinet before leaving himself.

I zipped up my jeans. *Great. This will be all over*

school by the end of first period.

"I apologize, Phil. I should've locked the door," the nurse said.

"That's okay," I said, but I didn't mean it. She had no idea the razzing I was going to take over this.

"Now, about your back." The nurse stripped off her gloves and tossed them into a trash can. "Most likely strained a muscle. Let's lie down for a while."

I shuffled to the bed, kicked off my sneakers and crawled on top of the covers.

"This should help." Nurse Johnson handed me a heating pad.

Lying face up, with the heating pad under my lower back, I folded my arms over my chest and closed my eyes. The nurse flipped off the lights on her way out and eased the door shut behind her.

I tried napping, but I kept picturing Loose Lips's startled expression when she spied my bare butt. Thanks to her, I'd be sure to take a razzing second hour. Of course, I was wide awake when Nurse Johnson came back three minutes before the end of first period.

"How's your back, Phil?" she asked.

"Right now it doesn't hurt."

"Let's see how you feel after you walk a bit."

I swung my legs over the side of the bed, shoved my sneakers on, slowly rose to my feet and took four baby steps. "Back feels fine."

"Excellent. Now let's get you to class."

I headed to the door.

"By the way, I called your mother and told her about your mishap," the nurse said. "I suggested you stay home this weekend and take it easy."

"Our family has a trip planned to Splash-City and a Milwaukee Brewers game."

"I'm afraid that's out. Maybe your family can go next weekend."

"I doubt it. Dad took off work, and we already bought the Splash-City tickets."

"Well, I hope things work out."

I sighed as I strode from the room. I should've gone ahead and flunked the test.

As I walked to social studies, C.J. fell into step beside me. "How did it go with the nurse?"

"Okay, except she called my mom and told her I shouldn't do anything this weekend."

"Aren't you going to Splash-City and a baseball game?"

"Supposed to leave Saturday morning. Hope I can talk my parents into letting me go."

As we ended our conversation, Loose Lips clomped past. "Nice butt, Dorkenstein."

"Go fart peas at the moon," I hollered at her as she walked away.

"What was that about?" C.J. said.

"Nothing," I said as we strolled into class.

Surprisingly, I didn't get teased much for the rest of the day. Loose Lips went home before second period began. The sight of blood oozing from her finger must've been too much for her.

✓ ✓ ✓

Later, as my parents and I ate a dinner of meat loaf and mashed potatoes, Mom told me about the call from the nurse.

"Yeah. I slipped getting off the bus. No biggie." I took a scoop of potatoes and dumped them onto my plate. The potatoes looked lumpy.

"That's not what the nurse told me. She said you needed to stay in the house this weekend and rest."

"Ma, it was no big deal. I'm fine."

"Your mother and I think it's best you stay with Grandma," Dad said, stuffing a hunk of meat loaf into his mouth.

"Why can't I just come along? I promise I won't go on any rides."

Dad swallowed his food and waved the fork at me. "The nurse said no, and we agree."

"Can't you change the dates?"

"I wish we could," Mom said, "but the hotel suite is nonrefundable."

"Plus it's impossible to exchange the Brewers

tickets," Dad said. "They were a gift from work."

I finished eating my dinner in silence and rose to leave.

"Don't you want a piece of chocolate cake?" Mom asked.

"No, thanks," I said. "Not really hungry."

I carried my plate and utensils to the counter and put them in the dishwasher. I left the kitchen in a huff and went up to my room.

That weekend, while my parents and my sister enjoyed themselves at the waterpark and the baseball game, I was confined to the house under my grandmother's watchful eye. With little to do, I studied my English notes and memorized the parts-of-speech section in the textbook.

On Monday, I took the test after school. I botched the part on prepositional phrases but still managed a B, my best English grade this year.

I guess studying does pay off.

RULE THREE

NEVER PULL THE HALFWAY CON ON A RAINY DAY

The Halfway Con was Shane Olson's idea.

I met Shane during my fifth week at Lost Creek. Our math class was discussing triangles when Principal Knox escorted Shane into the room. The principal introduced Shane to Mr. Fowler, shook Shane's hand and wished him luck.

After the principal left, Mr. Fowler stood, smoothed his striped tie and turned Shane to face the class."Kids, your attention, please. The young man standing beside me is Shane Olson from Madison, Wisconsin."

The newcomer didn't look like any sixth grader I knew. He wore a red University of Wisconsin Football T-shirt and white shorts. The blue-tinted wraparound sunglasses sitting on top of his long, straight blond hair struck me as pricey. His tan skin and worn leather sandals made him appear as if he'd come from the beach. About five feet tall and wiry, he stood straight as a flagpole, with his shoulders back and his chin up.

"Shane, tell us about yourself," Mr. Fowler said, "but first, ditch the sunglasses."

"Sure thing, Mr. Fowler." Shane removed his sunglasses and stowed them in his pocket. "As you can tell by my T-shirt, I'm a Badger fan. I like to play soccer, ride my skateboard and go camping."

He paused. His face tightened and his lips puckered as if he'd just eaten a dozen sour balls. Then his stomach growled and he put his hand on his belly and made an odd face. "*BURRRRRPPP*."

Mr. Fowler snickered. The girls giggled. The boys howled.

I laughed so hard a ginormous booger shot out my nose and flew across the aisle. When the booger landed on top of Abigail Utterback's blue sneaker, I almost busted a gut.

"Excuse me," Shane said after he got done laughing and the class had quieted down. "My favorite subjects are science and art. I'm pretty good at math, drawing and belching."

The class chuckled.

"Oh, yeah. Almost forgot. I live with my mom and my seven-year-old brother."

"Thanks for sharing, Shane," Mr. Fowler said. "For now, take a seat behind Phil." He pointed to me. "I'll assign you a seat tomorrow."

As Shane slid into the desk, Mr. Fowler checked the time. "Kids, class ends in three minutes. We'll resume our discussion on triangles tomorrow. You may talk until the bell, but keep the volume low."

I twisted around in my desk and stuck out my hand. "I'm Phil."

Shane gave me a hearty handshake. "Nice to meet you, Phil."

"That was the loudest burp ever," I said. "You sure cracked up class."

"Wasn't trying to be funny. The soda I gulped down on the way to school caught up with me."

"Trying or not, you were hilarious. My ribs hurt from laughing so much."

"Glad I didn't fart."

I chuckled. "Wish you had. I'd still be laughing."

The bell rang, signaling the end of third period. As everyone rose to leave, Mr. Fowler called Shane and me to his desk.

"Phil, Shane follows your class schedule. Take him to health and science and introduce him to his teachers. Then show him the ropes at lunch."

"Sure, Mr. Fowler," I said, proud he'd chosen me to be Shane's guide.

✓ ✓ ✓

A week later, I sat in English waiting for the day's announcements. While Ms. Joyner took attendance, my eyes panned the room until they rested on Shane's empty desk. Was he sick?

After announcements, most of us looked ready to fall asleep. Five or six kids had their heads down on their desks, and someone was snoring in the back.

Ms. Joyner raked her long fingernails across an old chalkboard. Everyone sat up.

"Now that you're all awake," she said, "let's have some fun."

Fun? There's a novel idea for Ms. Joyner.

"*Quick, strong* and *athletic* are words used to describe football players," Ms. Joyner said. "These words are called descriptive adjectives."

I perked up when she mentioned football. Maybe English would be bearable for once.

I couldn't have been more wrong. For the next half hour, Ms. Joyner babbled on about adjectives and never referred to football again.

As she wrapped up her droneathon, Shane

noisily swung the door open and waltzed into class.

Coming even a minute late to English was like poking a stick into a hornet's nest. Besides giving us the third degree, Ms. Joyner demanded we have a signed excuse. If we didn't, she kept us after school to make up the missed class time.

Ms. Joyner stopped class. "Before you sit down, Shane, I need to see your admittance slip and your excuse." Her tone left no question that she was unhappy.

"Sure," Shane said like a kid with no worries. He swaggered up to the teacher and handed her a crinkled note and an office admit slip.

Ms. Joyner glanced at the slip and read the note. "Take your seat, Shane," she said, "and let's work on being more responsible."

"Okay, Ms. Joyner." Shane headed to his seat, beaming as if he'd scored the winning touchdown in the Super Bowl.

After class, I caught up with Shane in the hallway. "How'd you do it?"

"Whaddya mean?"

"Joyner tears kids to pieces for being tardy. How did you get away with coming so late?"

“I used the halfway con.” Shane stopped at the drinking fountain and took a sip.

“What’s that?”

“A way of being late to school without getting hassled.” He wiped his mouth on his sleeve. “I use it when I need a break or if I forget to study for a first-period test.”

“How’s it work?” I asked, now curious.

“It’s simple. You need three things: a nice day, a parent who’s home but can’t take you to school and a signed excuse.”

“Sounds easy,” I said as we made our way to social studies. “Then what?”

“You accidentally-on-purpose leave something at home that you need for school, like your assignments or your books.”

“Go on,” I said, giving a wide berth to a girl busily texting on her way to class.

“Halfway to the bus stop, you remember your books. You head home, get your books and dawdle back to the bus stop. By the time you get back, the bus has left.”

Shane stooped down to pick up a quarter. “My lucky day.”

“So the bus is gone. Now what?” I asked Shane to get him back on track.

“You go home, get a signed excuse and hike

to school. If you walk slowly, you can miss first period."

"Why not take your bike?"

"Bike has a flat, duh."

"Sounds gutsy. Joyner could keep me after."

"Not if you have a signed excuse," Shane said as we strode into social studies. "Try it and see what happens, unless you're too scared."

I dumped my books on my desk. "I'm not scared! But with my luck, something's gotta go wrong."

"What could go wrong? Besides, if the con doesn't work, you make up the class time. Big deal."

"Okay, you win. I'll give it a shot next week."

✓ ✓ ✓

Egged on by Shane and needing a break from English, I tried the halfway con four days later.

I left my backpack in my room, ate breakfast and set off for school. When I stepped onto the front porch, I rested my elbows on the railing and sized up the day. A warm southerly breeze made it feel like July. Except for three large gray clouds blotting the sky in the distance, the day looked perfect.

I met C.J., who lived four blocks from me, at the end of his driveway and we headed to catch our bus. Halfway to the bus stop, I halted.

"Oh, great," I said. "Gotta go home. Forgot my

backpack." I made a U-turn and began retracing my steps.

"I'll save you a seat," C.J. called after me.

"Hope I'm back in time," I yelled back.

"Hope so, too," C.J. shouted, "before the rain comes." He pointed to the west.

I checked the sky behind me. The clouds I had seen earlier had doubled in size. They also appeared to be darker and closer. Not worried, I got out my Shuffle, put in my earbuds and hit "play" on my favorite playlist.

Three blocks later, the wind kicked up and the temperature dropped. I glanced behind me to see a jagged lightning bolt flash across the sky. Fast-moving storm clouds were headed in my direction.

If I turned around, I could still catch the bus, but all my assignments were at home. I'd take zeroes in every one of my classes.

I tucked my Shuffle and earbuds into my pants pocket and hustled home. By the time I veered onto the front walk, the sky had become pitch black and thunder rumbled overhead. While scampering onto the porch, I muttered a short prayer that I could catch the bus before the clouds let loose.

I unlocked the door and burst into the house. "It's me, Mom," I called out. "Forgot my backpack."

Mom stepped into the foyer wearing my father's

frayed flannel bathrobe. On her feet were my tattered tiger-paw animal slippers.

"Cute costume," I said, pounding up the stairs two at a time. "But isn't Halloween next week?"

"Funny, Phil, but I can't help you right now. Have to get ready for work."

"Just gotta grab my backpack," I hollered from the top of the stairs. I zipped into my room, chucked my Shuffle and earbuds onto the bed, threw on my backpack and tore down the stairs. On the last step, I stumbled, lost my balance and crashed into a tall skinny bookcase, sending books toppling from the top shelf.

"What was that?" Mom called from her bedroom.

"Nothing, Mom," I shouted back.

I raced out the front door, leaped from the porch and hit the walkway running. As I sprinted to the bus stop, a light drizzle began falling. This was going to be close.

When I reached the bus stop, I was out of breath—and out of luck. My ride was gone. I wheeled around, steamed at myself.

Next time, dummy, check the weather forecast.

By the fourth block of my trek home, the light drizzle had changed into a steady rain, and the wind started gusting. I took off running, sloshing through puddles on the slippery sidewalk. A block from my house, the monsoon struck. The gale-force winds and driving rain made the last block seem like a mile. Fallen pine needles whipped up by the wind pricked my face and arms.

After cutting across our soggy yard, I hurdled the dying lillies lining the narrow walkway and dashed under the porch's overhang. Soaked to the bone, I put my hands on my knees and caught my breath.

I let myself in and trudged up to my room. I peeled off my clothes, put on another outfit and headed downstairs.

Mom met me at the foot of the stairs. "What are you doing home?"

"Missed the bus. Can you give me a ride to school? It's pouring."

Mom crossed her arms over her chest. "Guess I'll have to, but it'll be fifteen minutes."

"Thanks, Mom. And I need a written excuse for being late." I went into the den and flipped on ESPN.

While watching football highlights, I got a text from C.J. "where ru?"

"missed bus. cu n english," I texted back.

SportsCenter was showing the last NFL highlight when Mom hollered, "Let's go."

I shut off the TV, crossed to the window and peered outside. Rain was coming down so hard I could barely see anything.

I followed Mom out the back door and into the garage. She pressed the garage door opener and the door slowly rolled up in its tracks. While Mom slid behind the wheel of our SUV, I tossed my backpack onto the back seat. I climbed into the passenger side and buckled up. Mom banged the door shut, adjusted her seat and strapped herself in.

"You realize this makes me late for work," she said as she handed me my excuse.

"Sorry, Mom, but I needed my books for school." I peeked at the excuse to make sure she had signed it and tucked the note in my pocket.

"How can you be so forgetful?" She jammed the key into the ignition and angrily turned the key. The SUV roared to life. She shoved the gearshift into reverse and stomped on the gas pedal. The SUV lurched backward and shot from the garage like a racehorse breaking out of the starting gate.

Realizing she was going too fast, Mom hit the brakes. The SUV skidded down the slick concrete driveway, swerved across the street and jumped the curb. We stopped with the SUV's rear wheels perched on the neighbor's newly planted lawn.

"You all right, Phil?" Mom asked, her voice full of concern.

"Fine." I forced myself not to laugh.

After putting the SUV in “park,” Mom tipped her head back against the headrest and took two slow, deep breaths. Regaining her composure, she hit the remote clipped to the sun visor. As the garage door closed, she turned on the wipers, put the SUV in “drive” and gunned the engine. The wheels spun in the soft dirt.

We were stuck.

Mom glared at me. “See what happens when you rush, Phil?”

Her tone made it clear she didn’t want an answer, so I buttoned my lips.

She cut the engine and tightly gripped the steering wheel with both hands. “You’ll have to ride your bike,” she said, gazing out the windshield.

“Can’t. Flat tire.” I unbuckled my seat belt.

Mom tapped her fingers on the steering wheel. “Still carry a windbreaker in your backpack?”

“Yeah.”

“Give it to me,” she snapped, unfastening her seat belt.

I grabbed my backpack and dug out the rumpled windbreaker. As I handed it to her, Mom pushed the door open. Holding the nylon jacket over her spiffy hairdo with both hands, she got out and shoved the door shut with her hip. As she dashed toward the house, the windbreaker flapped wildly above her head. But a gust of wind ripped it out of one hand while she scurried up the walkway. Within seconds, the rain had plastered her hair to her head.

Under the porch's roof, she chucked the windbreaker onto a wicker rocker and peered at the SUV. With her hair drooping over her face and ears, she looked like a cat after a bath. She yelled at me, but the rain pelting the windshield made it impossible to know what she said.

I didn't have to hear her, though. The way she formed her words so that her mouth exaggerated each syllable let me know she was furious.

After slipping off her muddy high heels, she whacked them together three times, unlocked the door and stormed into the house.

I hunkered down in the passenger seat and listened to the rain pummel the SUV's roof. *How am I getting to school?*

I didn't have to wait long for my answer.

Mom marched out the front door wearing Dad's hooded poncho and his rubber boots. She hurried toward the SUV with my sister's umbrella, the pink one with yellow ducks, clutched in her left hand. She flung open the driver's door and hurled the wrapped umbrella onto the driver's seat.

"Start walking."

"I can't take this umbrella. I'll look like a nerd."

Mom snatched her purse from the front seat and tucked the handbag under the poncho. "Get moving," she said before slamming the door shut and scooting back to the house.

I picked up my backpack by its straps, hopped from the SUV and found myself standing in muck. Leaving the umbrella on the seat, I closed the door and slung my backpack over my shoulders.

As I walked to school, I sloshed through puddles to clean my mud-caked sneakers. As I cut across the school playground, the rain tapered off, but by then I was sopping wet. Even my boxers were waterlogged.

At least I have a good excuse.

"Forget your umbrella, young man?" the secretary joked as I trudged into the office.

Too cold and wet to smile, I dug out my soggy excuse from my pocket. While handing the secretary my note, I noticed the ink had smeared.

"Please stand back," the secretary said. "You're dripping water on the counter."

I stepped back.

The secretary unfolded my note. "This is unreadable." She crumpled my excuse into a tiny ball. "I'll have to give you an unexcused absence."

"I know what the note says. Let me read it to you," I pleaded, shivering.

She didn't utter a word. Instead, she pitched my note into the wastebasket.

I stood with my shoulders hunched and gazed at my wet sneakers, ignoring the water trickling off my forehead and onto the floor. Without the note to give Ms. Joyner, I was sunk. Now, besides being late for school, I was also late for English. I'd have to stay after to make up the missed class time. I got drenched for no reason.

The secretary grabbed a pen and a pad of pink sticky notes lying on her desk. "What's your name and your mother's phone number?"

"Phil Abrams," I muttered without looking up. "My mother's work number is 739-6412."

The secretary wrote out an admit slip for English and set it on the counter. "I suggest you change into your gym clothes before going to class."

Too angry to respond, I plucked the admit slip off the counter and left. Having no other options, I heeded the secretary's advice and squished my way down the empty hallway to the locker room. While unlocking my locker, it dawned on me that I'd taken my gym clothes home to be washed.

I lumbered over to the Lost and Found box. The only items left were two ripped camouflage flip-flops, an extra-large, smelly "Go Frogs" T-shirt with a big hole in the side, a pair of small, ratty gym shorts, a dirty sweat sock and an old Boston Red Sox baseball cap.

I stripped off my wet clothes and soaked sneakers, pitched them into my locker and toweled off. I dried my boxers under the hand dryer as best I could and changed into my new getup.

As I left the locker room, I checked myself out in the long wall mirror. "Great," I muttered.

Dreading what was coming next, I dawdled to first period. I stopped by my locker, stashed my backpack and picked up my English materials. I made a detour into the bathroom and lingered a minute at the drinking fountain before heading to class.

I paused at the classroom door, slowly pushed down the handle and took a deep breath. *Rather be getting a tooth pulled.* Easing the door open, I stepped into the room.

Ms. Joyner stopped teaching and riveted her eyes on me, focusing the entire class on my plight. She glanced at the clock above the door before turning to me with a pained, scrunched-up look on her face. I'd seen this expression many times before. It's what my father looks like when he's constipated.

"Before you sit down, Phil, show me your admittance slip and your excuse," she said.

As I made my way across the room, I sensed that everyone was watching me. I felt as if I'd been caught jumping the line at the amusement park. I handed Ms. Joyner my admit slip.

"And where is your signed excuse, young man?"

"The secretary threw away my note because she couldn't read it." I thought I heard Shane snicker.

The teacher gave me an icy stare. "What's with the outfit?"

"My mother had an accident driving me to school. I had to hike here in the rain. I got these clothes out of Lost and Found."

"Is your mother okay?"

"She's fine."

"Glad to hear that. By the way, Phil, do you know when class starts?"

"Yes, Ms. Joyner."

"And what time might that be?" Her voice rose with each word.

"Seven fifty-five."

Ms. Joyner pushed her glasses up the bridge of her nose and checked her wristwatch. "It's 8:37." She tapped her watch for emphasis. "Forty-two minutes late times two. You owe me eighty-four minutes."

"But my mom got into an accident."

"You're still tardy. I'll see you after school. I'm also deducting ten points from your assignment, assuming it's done, for handing it in late."

I dragged myself to my desk, sat down and sighed.

After class, Shane met me at my locker. "Nice job, Dumbo."

"I told you something would go wrong."

"Yeah, you sure did." He glanced at my torn shirt and dinky shorts. "Love your new look."

That evening during dinner, my parents, to my surprise, didn't mention the accident. But when I got up to leave the table, my father stood, too. "Phil, let's go to your room and have a chat."

"Sure, Dad." I groaned because these father-son chats never ended well for me.

When we got to my room, I flopped down on my unmade bed. My father remained standing. "Well, son, see what happens when a person is irresponsible?"

"Yeah, Mom really burnt some rubber leaving the garage." I chuckled.

Dad drummed his fingers against his thigh. "I'm not talking about your mother, son, and I don't find this a bit funny."

"But I didn't cause the accident! Mom's the one

who peeled out of the garage."

"Your mother was rushing because she wanted to be on time for work. Last month when she was late, her boss chewed her out."

I stared at my father. "It's my fault?"

Dad sat on the edge of the bed next to me. "In a way, yes. If you remember your books, the accident doesn't happen. And your mother wouldn't have wasted half a vacation day waiting for a tow truck."

"Dad, if being forgetful caused accidents, there'd be millions a day."

"I'm not getting into a debate about this, son. I've already decided how I'm handling this. Topsoil and a tow truck cost close to a hundred dollars."

"A hundred bucks?" I said, dumbfounded.

"Tow trucks are expensive, and topsoil isn't cheap either."

"Don't we have insurance?"

"We do, but if we submit a claim this small, our rates will go up."

"So you have to cough up a hundred bucks?"

Dad's phone buzzed loudly in his pocket. He ignored it. "No, I have to shell out fifty bucks. Because you're half at fault, you'll pay the other half."

"Half! I haven't got five bucks to my name."

"I know it's a lot of money, but you need to

be taught that being irresponsible has a price. I'll deduct two dollars from your allowance each week. You'll have your share paid off in no time."

"Dad, that's not fair."

He stood and headed for the door. Apparently, our conversation was over.

"Sometimes life isn't fair, son," my father said as he strode from the room.

I did the math in my head. Paid off in no time. Who was my father kidding? Since it was October, I'd make my last payment sometime in April.

After spending the evening doing homework, I pulled out my Rules of Never notebook out of my desk drawer, grabbed a pen and got into bed. Propping myself against the headboard, I reflected on my ill-fated attempt at the halfway con.

I concluded the con was still a good idea if one sticks to the rules, especially the rule about checking the weather forecast. I opened the notebook to the third page and on the first line jotted down Rule Three: "NEVER PULL THE HALFWAY CON ON A RAINY DAY." I set the notebook on the nightstand and switched off the lamp.

I drifted off to sleep, mad at everybody: the secretary for not accepting my excuse, Ms. Joyner for making me stay after, my father for making me pay for the accident and myself for being so dumb.

RULE FOUR

NEVER MISS A CHANCE TO GET EVEN

Most teachers have a good side and a bad side. Not the ancient Terrance Fry. His sides were worse and worser.

Mr. Fry taught health, which was a joke because he was the unhealthiest person I knew. He smoked like a chimney and looked like a walrus. Only by turning sideways was he able to squeeze through his classroom door. Nicknamed “Wide Track” by students, he didn’t walk—he waddled.

It would be kind to call Wide Track bald because the top of his egg-shaped head was a series of shiny bumps and dents. To hide his hair loss, he combed over the long, gray strands of hair on each side of his head. Some days he brushed the stringy strands from left to right, other days right to left. Neither way worked.

On the way to health one morning, C.J. and I joked about Wide Track's comical effort at hiding his bald dome. "Betcha a quarter he combed his hair left to right," I said.

"What are ya, psychic?" C.J. asked, a hint of sarcasm in his voice.

"No, just a hunch."

"Call that a hunch? You gotta fifty-fifty chance of being right."

"Then bet me, or are ya chicken?" I gave him a gentle shove.

"You're on." He shoved me back. "Can't wait to wipe that smirk off your face."

"Be prepared to lose a quarter," I said as we entered the room.

Wide Track was leaning against the corner of his king-size wooden desk dressed like a funeral director. The bored expression on his deeply lined face told me he wished he were someplace else.

The room's decor matched the teacher's clothes: drab. No potted plants. No inspiring health posters. No eye-catching displays. No outside light from the room's puny window because Wide Track kept the blinds drawn. Students called the room "Gloom and Doom."

C.J. frowned when he spotted Wide Track's head. Sure enough, the last few strands were combed left to right.

"Better luck next time." I gently elbowed C.J. in the ribs. "Now, fork over my quarter."

C.J. slowly dug into his pants pocket and fished out a dime and three nickels. "Here." He slapped the coins into my hand. "Just lucky, Phil."

"Mr. Pouty Face can't stand losing twenty-five cents."

C.J. opened his mouth to say something, but before he could, the bell rang.

"Everyone be seated," Wide Track directed as he settled into the chair behind his desk. The chair creaked under his weight.

Wide Track ran health like a Marine boot camp. He was the drill sergeant and we were his recruits. In his room, fun and learning never mixed, making health duller than a lecture on head lice.

Wide Track never laughed. When he smiled, which was seldom, his crooked teeth showed and his chin jutted out, making him appear even more unpleasant. At least he didn't play favorites. He disliked everyone.

Besides being boring, we resented him for another reason: his wicked temper. Kids would rather be locked in a closet with a pile of rattlesnakes than face Mr. Fry's wrath. Students got chewed out, or "Fried," for the most trivial reasons, like not having a Number 2 pencil.

Midway through class, Wide Track reached into his desk drawer and pulled out a short stack of yellowed index cards held together by two fat rubber bands. "Get out your notebooks."

I suddenly realized I needed to get rid of the bubble gum I'd popped into my mouth in science. Not only had the gum lost its flavor, but more important, if Wide Track caught me, I'd get Fried. I took out a battered health notebook and a pencil, making sure it was a Number 2.

After removing the rubber bands, Wide Track organized the cards, licked his fingertips and reeled off facts on nutrition. Data poured from his mouth like quarters from a slot machine. I wrote furiously but found it impossible to keep up.

Finally, Wide Track paused, giving my fingers a much-needed rest. "Any questions before I give you your assignment?" He scanned his bored audience searching for a raised hand.

Now was the time to ditch the gum. As Wide Track panned the other side of the room, I yawned and cupped my hand over my mouth. I tongued the gum into my palm and slipped the wad under the seat of my desk.

But I was too slow. Out of the corner of my eye, I saw Wide Track slap the index cards down on his desk.

I sat up as he removed the wire-rim glasses perched on his broad hooked nose. His weather-beaten face grew beet red, like it might burst into flames.

"Abrams, front and center." Most teachers call students by their last names to show their displeasure. Not Wide Track. He *always* called us by our last names. He told us he wanted to keep class formal, but I figured he'd never cared to learn our first names.

The class let out a collective gasp. An eerie stillness filled the room, like in a cemetery at midnight. Fitting, since I was now dead meat.

Nervous as a turtle in a shark tank, I plodded up to face Wide Track. I stood ramrod straight in front of his desk trying to keep my breathing normal, waiting for him to unload. I felt alone even though twenty-six students sat behind me. I couldn't see them, but I knew their eyes were fixed on Wide Track's next victim.

"Were you chewing gum, Abrams?" The

teacher's thundering voice shattered the room's silence. He tightened his jaw, furrowed his brow and glared at me.

"Yes, Mr. Fry." Getting caught lying to Wide Track was worse than being Fried.

"You do know, Abrams, chewing gum is forbidden in my room, don't you?" Wide Track's crooked teeth seemed awfully large but not as large as the veins bulging out of his flabby neck.

"Yes." My knees trembled. I sank my hands into my pockets to keep them from shaking.

"Let me get this straight." Wide Track's blazing eyes narrowed. "You knew the rule, yet you still broke it. Is that correct, Abrams?" Veins pulsed in anger on the teacher's neck.

"Not really, Mr. Fry." I tried to keep my voice steady. "I forgot to throw the gum away before class." A feeble excuse but the truth.

As steam rose from the top of his head, Wide Track exploded like a hundred sticks of dynamite. "So that's your explanation! You forgot! And once you remembered, you tried hiding the gum underneath your desk!"

Droplets of sweat trickled down the sides of my body as his voice boomed off the concrete block walls and echoed throughout the room.

"Well, let me tell you about obeying the rules and the destruction of public property." Spit splattered on and over his desk. I inched backward to keep from getting sprayed.

As he tore into me, I pondered his "destruction of public property" comment. If Hubba Bubba can wreck a desk, what had the gum done to my teeth?

"You will report here tomorrow after school and scrape all the gum from underneath your desk. Is that clear, Abrams?"

"Yes, Mr. Fry." *Yeah, whatever.*

"Now take your seat." Wide Track put on his glasses and gathered up the index cards.

As I slid into my desk, I muttered to Jenna, who sat across from me. "Health is the pits."

Wide Track slid his glasses midway down the bridge of his nose and peered at me over the rims. "What did you say, Abrams?"

"Nothing, Mr. Fry."

"Did you say health is the pits?" he asked in a harsh tone.

"No. I told Jenna my boxers were giving me fits."

The class chuckled.

As he drummed his fingertips on his desk, Wide Track stared straight at me with his beady eyes.

Was he deciding whether to punish me for my smart-alecky comment?

"I've changed my mind, Abrams," he snarled. "You'll clean every desk in this room."

I dropped my head. Tomorrow was going to be a long day.

"The assignment is written on the front board," Wide Track said. "Now everyone get to work."

I flipped to Page 78 in the textbook and answered the chapter questions. The longer I worked on my assignment, the more steamed I got. I'd had enough of the tyrant's strict rules.

When Wide Track was distracted, I reached under my desk, removed the wad of gum and popped it into my mouth. I chewed slowly and carefully until the bell rang.

C.J. and Shane caught up with me in the hallway after class.

"Sweet, Phil," C.J. said. "Wide Track totally flipped out."

"He sure did," Shane chimed in. "That was a zillion times more exciting than your phone going off last week."

"Are those *compliments*, guys? I wasn't trying to set a record." I spit my gum into the garbage and noticed that it was purple.

"I saw you stick your gum under the desk," C.J.

said. "Did you take out a fresh piece?"

"Nope," I said. "When Wide Track wasn't looking, I grabbed my ABC gum."

"What kinda gum is that?" Shane said.

"Already been chewed."

"Gross," C.J. said.

"You've got more guts than me," Shane said. "If Wide Track would've caught you chewing gum twice in the same class, you'd have detention for a month."

"You guys don't know the half of it," I said.

"Whaddya talkin' about?" C.J. asked.

"The gum I put in my mouth wasn't mine."

"Yuck!" C.J. made a disgusted face.

"Probably catch some nasty disease," I said.

"At least you won't have to go to school." Shane chuckled.

"How did it taste?" C.J. asked.

"Like a gummy worm," I said. "How do ya think?"

As the three of us headed to our lockers, I stopped at the drinking fountain and rinsed out my mouth.

The next day, under Wide Track's supervision, I scraped gum from twenty-seven desks using his putty knife. Eighty-seven minutes later, I finished.

"Thank you, Abrams," Wide Track said as I

handed him the knife. "I've wanted those desks cleaned for years."

"You're welcome, Mr. Fry." I left the room hoping that someday I could repay him.

A week later, I got my chance.

While I was in the library half-listening to Mr. Patterson explain our social studies project, my eyes strayed around the room. When I spotted a TV remote lying beneath an empty book cart, a flash of inspiration hit me.

I weighed the consequences of swiping the remote. If I was caught, a three-day suspension would be the least of my problems. I decided that getting even with Wide Track was worth the risk.

As our class left the library, I dropped my pencil near the book cart. When I crouched down to pick up my pencil, I snatched the remote and slid it into my binder. I tucked the binder under my arm and rejoined my classmates.

Four days later, I struck.

After taking attendance, Wide Track surveyed the room to make sure he had our undivided attention. "Kids, the DVD you're about to watch on flossing will last the entire period. I expect you to take notes on the important points. We will discuss the DVD tomorrow."

I got out a spiral bound notebook, removed the pencil nub wedged inside the wire loops and slapped the notebook onto my desk.

After starting the disk, Wide Track flipped off the lights, plodded to the back of the room and parked himself in a metal folding chair. I made myself as comfy as possible and opened my notebook. I thumbed through it until I found a blank page and got ready to write.

On the monitor, a wide-faced man with a short bumpy nose and wearing a white lab coat stood next to a large poster of a toothy smile that read, "Teeth Love To Be Flossed." He introduced himself in a whining monotone. "Hi, boys and girls. I'm Dentist Dave and I'm here to talk about the importance of flossing."

I rolled my eyes. "WHOOP-DE-DO," I wrote on the top of the page.

Dentist Dave continued. "Why should a person floss every day? The first reason is that flossing prevents tartar buildup." I tuned him out. I did *not* need to know that—ever.

As Dentist Dave explained the second reason, the prevention of gum disease, I peeked behind me. I was out of Wide Track's sight line. I sank down in my desk, folded my hands in my lap, tipped my head back and closed my eyes. Nap time.

I tried dozing, but the monitor was only eight feet away and its glare lit me up like a lighthouse beacon. Since snoozing was no longer an option, I leaned over and picked up my binder. Carefully, I removed the remote and slid it under my desktop. I aimed it at the monitor and hit the power button.

The screen went dark.

Wide Track grunted twice and made his way like a three-toed sloth to the monitor and pressed the "on" button.

I waited until he returned to his seat and struck again.

"What in blazes?" Wide Track grunted again, rose to his feet and lumbered to the monitor.

C.J., who knew I had the remote, blurted out, "The monitor must be busted, Mr. Fry."

"These monitors never work," Wide Track muttered.

As he reached for the remote Velcroed to the DVD player, I switched the monitor on. Muttering again, he snatched the remote and slogged back to his seat.

Once he got settled, I pressed the power button for the fourth time. When the screen went blank, Wide Track heaved himself to his feet, trudged to the center of the room, aimed the remote and pushed the power button. The monitor sprang to life.

I sneaked a peek at C.J., who was biting his lower lip to keep from laughing, and hit the "off" button.

Wide Track switched the monitor on.

I turned the volume to the max.

He turned the volume down.

I cut the power to the monitor.

Wide Track dragged himself to the front of the room, all the while shaking his head. He set the remote on the DVD player and faced the class, rocking back and forth on his heels. His neck muscles tightened and the corner of his mouth twitched.

"I give up," he announced and pushed the monitor out of the way. He waddled to his desk, slid open the bottom drawer and pulled out a bunch of papers. "Since I have nothing else planned for class, you will work on this."

Holding a stack of worksheets high above his head, he motioned to Jenna with his wrinkled hand. "Pass these out."

Jenna stopped rolling her pencil across her desk, stood and snatched the worksheets. While she passed out our homework, I slipped the remote into my binder.

I cracked a smile while working on my assignment and scribbled the answer to the last question as the bell chimed, signaling the end of class.

C.J. caught up with me at my locker. "That's one of the gutsiest things I've ever seen."

"Now Wide Track and I are even."

"You better hope he never finds out you have a remote."

"If he does, you blabbed, 'cause you're the only one besides me who knows."

"I won't tell anybody. I swear," C.J. said, crossing his heart.

Two weeks later, health class ended. Seeing no reason to keep the remote, I went to the library and sneaked it onto a bookshelf, near where I'd found it. The remote had served its purpose.

RULE FIVE

NEVER EAT CHILI THE NIGHT BEFORE SCHOOL

Cramps—horrible, twisting, gut-wrenching stomach cramps.

I'd been feeling off since scrambling out of bed that morning—I'd probably eaten too many helpings of Dad's Texas chili for dinner. After making three trips to the bathroom during the night, I had a hard time waking up.

With no time to shower, I splashed cold water on my face, put on an extra layer of deodorant and got ready for school. I grabbed my backpack and flew downstairs. Hurrying into the kitchen, I ran smack-dab into my annoying little sister.

"Watch where you're going, pinhead," Kaylee squawked. "I almost spilled my Frosted Flakes."

"Wearing them would be an improvement, fishface," I shot back, raising my voice.

Kaylee made an ugly face and stuck out her tongue.

"Cut it out, you two." Mom stepped between us. "You're running late, Phil."

"Fell back to sleep." I set my backpack on the floor next to the island counter and poured myself a small glass of freshly squeezed orange juice.

Mom tightened her apron strings. "There's toast your father didn't eat."

I plucked the slice of burned rye bread from the toaster. No wonder Dad didn't want it. Leaning over the sink so it caught the crumbs, I snapped the cold toast in half. I buttered one piece, stuffed it into my mouth and threw the other half into the disposal. I guzzled down the OJ to wash away the charred taste and set the glass in the dishwasher before Mom reminded me.

I went to the fridge and grabbed my lunch. As usual, the brown paper bag had "PA" scrawled in black marker on one side. I hated it when Mom wrote my initials on the bag. It reminded me of kindergarten, when she'd printed my name in bold capital letters on my Thomas the Train lunch box.

As I squeezed the bag into my backpack, Mom patted the back of a chair at the end of the table. "Eat a bowl of cereal."

"Can't, Mom. Gotta motor or I'll miss the bus."

"At least tie your shoes."

I tied my sneakers, threw on my hoodie and scooped up my backpack. "See ya, Mom," I shouted as I bolted out the back door. If the bus was running late, I might catch it.

Minutes later, panting like a racehorse and sweating like one, I reached the bus stop. With my heart racing, I waved madly as the school bus drove off.

Luckily, the driver caught sight of me. After pulling the bus to the curb and turning on the flashing red lights, he opened the door as I dashed up to the bus. Winded, I caught my breath and stepped aboard. The door slapped shut behind me.

"Thanks for stopping," I said.

"You're welcome, Phil. Tomorrow, get up earlier," the driver said half-jokingly.

"I'll try," I said, amazed he knew my name.

I made my way down the aisle and found an empty seat next to a pale freckle-faced girl I'd never seen before. Her fiery shoulder-length red hair matched the color of her ping-pong-ball-size earrings and the nail polish on her extra-long fingernails. "Mind if I sit here?"

She blew the strands of hair away from her face and parted her lips as if she wanted to say something, but didn't. Instead, she picked up a multicolored backpack on the seat next to her and set it on her lap. Her scowl told me why the spot had remained vacant.

"Thanks," I said, ending our one-way conversation. She shot me a look that warned me not to bother her again.

I slipped off my backpack and plopped down on the lumpy vinyl seat thinking how lucky I was to have caught the bus.

Before long, though, I didn't feel so lucky.

On the way to school, the driver was doing his best to hit as many bumps and potholes as possible. Each time he did, the impact stirred up last night's chili. By the time I stepped off the bus in the parking lot, I felt as if I'd swallowed a swarm of bumblebees.

Hurrying into school, I checked the hallway clock. Since my bus arrived late, I had four minutes to go to my locker, stop at the bathroom and get to English. I shoved my backpack into my locker, grabbed my English book and my binder and dashed down the hallway. I skipped my badly needed visit to the bathroom. I didn't want to be tardy for first period and face Ms. Joyner's wrath.

I'll hold it and go after class.

For some reason, rushing to beat the bell soothed my stomach. By the time Ms. Joyner took attendance and read the day's announcements, the bees had settled down. And when it was time to move on to social studies, the bees were a distant memory.

I loved social studies, and what made class special was the teacher, Mr. Patterson. He told cool stories, goofed around during class, enjoyed talking sports and had a great sense of humor. He treated everyone with respect and encouraged us to do our best.

In his late thirties, Mr. P was a skinny guy, and with his thick, coal-black hair, he always looked as if he'd driven through a hurricane on his way to school. Mr. P never taught in a sport jacket and seldom put on a necktie. Every casual Friday, he wore a crazy-colored bowling shirt, faded jeans and flashy red bowling shoes.

Today, Mr. P began class with a question. "Kids, before beginning today's lesson, I need an answer to something that has been puzzling me since I started teaching at Lost Creek. I often drive past Fort Howard Cemetery on the way to school. Does anyone know how many dead people are buried there?"

"It's a big cemetery, Mr. P," Shane said. "I'd say about a thousand."

"It has more than that, at least twenty-five hundred," C.J. said.

"If you want to know the exact number, Google it," I suggested.

"It's not important," Mr. P said. "Besides, I know the answer." His face broke into a grin as if the key word needed to complete a crossword puzzle had popped into his head.

"What is it?" I asked.

"All of them." Mr. P beamed. "Gotcha." He slapped his thigh and chuckled.

The class moaned.

"Mr. P," I said. "Why does a milking stool have three legs?"

He scratched the side of his head. "No idea, Phil."

"Because the cow has the udder."

The teacher slowly shook his head. "Good one, Phil."

"Mr. P," Shane blurted out. "Why are soccer players never invited to dinner?"

"Got me, Shane."

"Because they're always dribbling."

Everyone groaned.

C.J. raised his hand. "I got one."

"No more jokes," Mr. P said. "Otherwise, we won't get anything done." He rolled up his sleeves. "Now take out your social studies book and turn to the page written on the top right corner of the board."

Twenty-seven students got out their textbooks, flipped through the pages and stopped on Page 86: "Regions of the United States."

"As you see by the map on Page 86, the United States is divided into five regions: the Northeast, Southeast, Midwest, Southwest and West," Mr. P said. For thirteen minutes, he touched on how each region was unique but also part of the country.

As Mr. P discussed the last region, Dad's Texas chili began percolating.

Mr. P moved to the front of the room. Using the Smart Board, he showed us a physical map of the United States. "Let's review the major physical features within the five regions."

Using his index finger as a pen, he outlined the eastern coastline. "What body of water lies next to the East Coast?"

"The Atlantic Ocean," a girl called out from

the third row.

"Correct, Diane," Mr. P said. "The Atlantic is the second-largest ocean in the world. Anyone know the largest?"

"The Pacific," answered a boy seated next to Diane.

"Nice job, Bill," Mr. P said.

My gut churned.

Working his way west, Mr. P highlighted a line of mountains. "Can anyone name the mountain range running through the Northeast and Southeast regions?"

A girl four seats over raised her hand. "The Appalachians."

Waves of pain shot through my stomach. *Will this lesson ever end?*

"Well done, Nora." Mr. P circled five large lakes in the Northeast and Midwest regions. "Now, who can name the Great Lakes?"

"I can," Nicole said eagerly.

"Okay, Nicole. Let's start here." Mr. P pointed to the easternmost lake.

Oh, great—he's going through all five.

"Ontario," Nicole answered. Before Mr. P had a chance to point to the next lake, Nicole recited the other four. "Next to Ontario is Erie, above Erie is Huron, west of Huron is Michigan and the last lake is Superior."

Dad's chili was now staging a full-scale revolt. I folded my arms across my stomach and hunched over with my head down, hoping the pain would disappear.

Instead, it got worse. I should have left the room three minutes ago, but Mr. P had made it clear from Day One that nobody left class while he taught.

"Excellent, Nicole." Mr. P clapped his hands.

Now was my chance to ask to go to the bathroom.

I started to raise my hand, but Mr. P rambled on. "Class, what river splits the country in half?" He drew a red line from Minnesota's southeastern border to the Gulf of Mexico.

A girl somewhere behind me shouted, "The Mississippi."

"Great answer, Sandra," Mr. P said. "Class, here's a harder one. Name the plains west of the Mississippi River." He drew a circle around a large area.

Won't the man ever stop? This is urgent—I'm in agony here.

The question stumped the class. Me, I didn't care. My mind was down south.

"Two hints," Mr. P said. "It lies mostly in the Midwest region and its initials are G.P."

While my classmates racked their brains for the answer, the gas in my gut threatened to explode. My first impulse was to release the gas all at once. I pictured the blast peeling the paint off the walls and blowing a hole in my jeans. I'd feel a whole lot better, but the janitor would have to repaint the room. I'd also be walking to math with a softball-size hole in my pants and reeking like a dirty diaper.

C.J. raised his hand.

"Okay, C.J., what's the answer?" Mr. P said.

"The Great Pains," C.J. joked. "I mean the Great Plains."

I clutched my belly and silently released my first bomb.

When the smell hit my nostrils, I quickly put my hand over my mouth and nose. The fart stunk worse than usual. Dad once mentioned that life was a barrel of surprises. I hoped my classmates enjoyed my surprise.

As the putrid odor drifted through the classroom, I joined them in panning the room to see who the culprit was. When I turned my attention back to the Smart Board, I began to break wind every thirty seconds. But after easing out my fourth bomb, timing each one became impossible.

My classmates soon figured out that I was the Brown Bomber.

"Way to go, Abrams," a guy hollered from the middle of the room.

"That last bomb almost put me in the hospital, Phil," C.J. shot out from the back of the second row.

With a sheepish smile, I turned around and saw everyone staring at me with crinkled noses and disgusted looks on their faces.

Mr. P wrapped up his lesson and gave us an assignment to work on in class. As he plunked himself down in his chair, I sprang from my seat and made a beeline to the teacher's desk. "Can I go to the bathroom, Mr. P? I gotta go bad."

Getting a whiff of the foul odor hovering around him like a cloud, Mr. P pinched his nose. "Yes, Phil. Please go before I keel over."

Kids sitting near Mr. P chuckled.

"Thanks a million." I spun around to leave.

"Phil, don't forget your hall pass." Mr. P cranked open the window behind him, letting in cold, fresh air.

I plucked the orange wooden frog from a hook on the sidewall and bolted from the room. I booked down the hallway at warp speed and scooted into the bathroom, where I darted into the first stall. Within seconds, I felt a bajillion times better. Thank goodness my jeans were the kind with a zipper. If I'd been wearing button-fly jeans, I would have pooped my pants.

Letting out a big sigh of relief, I flushed the toilet. *If I ever need a laxative, I'll just eat Dad's chili.* As I sauntered out of the stall to wash my hands, I hiked up my jeans and zipped them, but the zipper stuck. I tugged and tugged—it wouldn't budge. I tried covering the zipper with my Packers T-shirt, but the shirt was too short.

"Now what am I gonna do?" I asked my reflection in the mirror. "I can't go back to class."

I stood near the sinks waiting for a classmate from social studies to show up, but I soon grew tired of standing. I pushed open the door to the middle stall, slipped in and took a seat on a dingy toilet. Propping open the door with my knee, I waited to be rescued.

To pass the time, I read dozens of scrawled notes on the stall's walls. Time dragged by. Finally, as I finished the last note, Shane strolled past the stall and did a double take.

"Uh, Mr. P sent me to see if you'd fallen in," he said.

"'Bout time. Could've read a novel."

"Can I ask a stupid question?"

"The way my day's going, why not?"

"Why are you sitting on a toilet?"

"My zipper's stuck and I got tired of standing waiting for help."

Shane almost split a gut laughing.

I waited for him to stop shaking. "You have to go and ask Mr. P for a safety pin."

"A safety pin? What for?"

"So I can pin my zipper together. Duh."

"Gotcha. Be back in a jiffy." He turned to leave. "Don't go anywhere."

"Thanks for the advice. The last thing I'm gonna do is cruise around with my zipper wide open."

Shane left chuckling.

I hunkered down on the toilet. With no more notes to read, I amused myself by performing "Itsy Bitsy Spider." The spider was climbing up the waterspout for the fifth time when Shane returned.

"Mr. P didn't have a safety pin, so he asked the class for one," he said.

I leaped to my feet and stood in the stall doorway. "He did *what*?"

"He wanted to find out if anyone had a safety pin. Veronika Painter had one in her pencil case, but she'd only give me the pin if I told her why I needed it. So I told her."

"You told the Booger Princess? Now the whole class knows."

"I said you lost a button on your shirt, but she

didn't buy my story."

"Great. Now I'll get ripped on all morning."

"Yeah, but at least your zipper will stay shut." Shane handed me the safety pin.

After inspecting the pin for boogers, I pinned my zipper together and stretched my T-shirt over it as far as possible. As ready as I was ever going to be, I headed back to social studies with Shane.

"Wait here a sec," he told me as he swung open the classroom door. With his head poked into the room, he announced, "Stinky Pants is back."

When I walked in, my classmates broke into applause. After taking a bow, I strolled over and hung up the hall pass.

"Phil, can I see you a sec?" Mr P said, and I walked up to his desk. He reached into his bottom drawer. "I got this years ago for my ski jacket and thought you could use it." He pulled out a heavy-duty zipper and handed it to me.

The room shook with laughter.

"No thanks, Mr. P," I said. "The safety pin will work just fine."

As I crossed the room to my desk, the boys in the front row and I exchanged high-fives. I sat down not knowing if I should be embarrassed or proud.

Stinky Pants.

The nickname stuck.

RULE SIX

NEVER FORGET YOUR FRIENDS

Chair 14 was the last chair in the trumpet section. Mrs. Murray, our band director, sat members of each section by playing ability. The student who played the instrument the best earned the honor of sitting in first chair. The student who played the second best sat in the second chair and so on.

After listening to my trumpet audition during the first week of school, Mrs. Murray plopped me in the last chair. But sitting at the end of the section didn't bother me, because:

- Mrs. Murray was an excellent teacher.

- Mrs. Murray was an easy grader.
- And I deserved the last spot.

To play the trumpet well, a person's cheeks had to remain tight. I looked like a chipmunk with its cheeks stuffed with acorns.

Mrs. Murray made it clear just how bad I was when I moseyed into band one afternoon and found a chair wedged between Olivia Overstreet and myself.

"Mrs. Murray, why the extra chair in our row?" I asked after class. "Did Olivia say something to you?"

"No. Should she have?"

When I didn't reply, Mrs. Murray said, "We're getting a new trumpet player on Friday, and I have no time to audition her until next week."

"Gotcha, but why is the chair between us?"

"I needed to add a chair to your row. Don't take this the wrong way, Phil, but I just assumed she plays the trumpet better than you."

"No problem, Mrs. Murray," I said. "So now I'm sitting in Chair 14?"

"Correct."

"Great," I said. "Fourteen is my lucky number."

On Friday, Susan from Ohio sat in Chair 13. Mrs. Murray's hunch was right: she played better than me.

Although horrible at the trumpet, I was breezing through band with a B, thanks to Mrs. Murray's generosity. But then it all changed three days before the end of first semester. That's when Mrs. Murray passed out sheet music for "Rudolph the Red-Nosed Reindeer."

"Kids, your attention please," she said, standing on the podium in front of the room. She tapped her baton against her steel music stand.

Everyone stopped talking.

"I know this is a departure from past years, but I'm testing each of you, either tomorrow or Friday. Your performance will count for one-half of your semester grade."

The entire class groaned, and then we all started grumbling and complaining.

Mrs. Murray rapped her baton against the music stand. "Quiet please!"

The room fell silent.

"You each have a part for 'Rudolph the Red-Nosed Reindeer.' You may pick the section you wish to perform, but your solo must be memorized and last at least twenty-five seconds."

"Why a test?" a drummer from the back of the room called out.

"To be frank," Mrs. Murray said, "I've received a lot of criticism that band is too easy."

"That's why I took band," the drummer said. "No stress."

"I understand, but I'm giving testing a shot this semester."

The grumbling and complaining grew louder.

A tuba player aired his gripe. "Mrs. Murray, we already have enough semester tests."

"I'll say," piped up a guy from the saxophone section.

"Tell you what," Mrs. Murray said, "I'll compromise. The performance score will count for one-fourth of your semester grade rather than half."

The grumbling died down into some muttering, several shrugs and even five or six nods of approval.

"What sections are testing Thursday?" C.J. asked. He also played trumpet, and he sat in the seventh chair, right in front of me.

"I don't know the order, but I will test half the class each day. Flutes, clarinets, trumpets and saxophones will perform tomorrow."

"What happens if you're sick?" a trombone player hollered. Before Mrs. Murray had a chance to answer the question, the bell rang.

✓ ✓ ✓

That night after finishing my math and science homework, I planned to practice and memorize my trumpet solo. But when I searched for my sheet music in my math folder, the paper was missing. Then I remembered I'd given it to C.J. to hold after band. He must have forgotten to give it back.

I called him at home, but his mom told me he'd gone to a hockey game with his father. When I buzzed him on his phone, he didn't answer. I texted him to call me ASAP. I waited until ten o'clock, but he never called.

There goes my B.

The next morning I met C.J. at the bus stop. "Why didn't you call me back last night?"

"Got home too late. The hockey game went into overtime."

"Could've texted me from the game."

"Didn't have my phone. What did ya want?"

"Remember yesterday after band when I handed you my sheet music?"

"Yeah."

"I think you still have it."

"I *do*?" He dug into his backpack and pulled out his science folder. He opened the folder and took out two sheets of music.

"Figured I got an extra one by mistake. Sorry,

Phil. You want it?"

"Keep it. I can't possibly memorize my solo by this afternoon."

✓ ✓ ✓

After lunch, I dragged myself into band. Most of the kids, including C.J., were in their chairs warming up. The sound of eighty-some kids all playing different parts of "Rudolph the Red-Nosed Reindeer" out of sync was earsplitting.

When C.J. spotted me, he shouted over the noise, "Got ya covered, Phil."

"Whaddya mean?"

Before he could explain, Mrs. Murray marched up to the podium and tapped her baton against the music stand. "Let's get started."

My stomach churned as I sat down on the metal folding chair. Since I had no chance of passing the test, I left my trumpet in its case.

Once everyone settled down, testing began. The clarinets went first, the flutes second. By the time the last flute finished her solo, close to two dozen renditions of "Rudolph" had been performed, most of them dreadful.

The sides of my head throbbed, making it hard to pay attention. I glanced at the clock on the front wall: 1:21. Not even halfway through class.

Mrs. Murray moved on to the trumpets.

The boy in the first chair performed, followed by the girl in the second. After C.J. blew his final note, Mrs. Murray went on to our row.

As the eighth chair played her solo, C.J. pulled off his sweatshirt, and I did a double take. He'd pinned my sheet music to the back of his "Frogs Rule" T-shirt.

I hurriedly opened my case and removed my trumpet. My hands shook so much that I fumbled with attaching the mouthpiece.

Five solos later, Chair 13 performed.

"Okay, Phil, you're up," Mrs. Murray said.

I stood.

Focusing on C.J.'s back, I put the mouthpiece to my lips, took a deep breath, puffed up my cheeks and blew, awaiting the first sour note. It never came. Instead, a shrill, piercing sound echoed through the room. Fire alarm!

The deafening blare made my ears ring.

Mrs. Murray struggled to be heard. "You know the drill, kids. We leave by rows," she said in a clear, calm and loud voice. "The percussion section will file out first. Flutes last. Last one out turns off the lights and closes the door. No talking."

Students stood, set their instruments on their chairs and waited their turn to leave. After C.J. set his trumpet down, he pulled his sweatshirt over his head and led his row from the room. Our row left next. We silently exited the room in single file, hustled down the hallway and walked out the door to the parking lot. When all the band members were safely outside, Mrs. Murray took roll.

While everyone waited for the fire department to arrive, I tracked C.J. down.

"Thanks for bailing me out," I said. "You took quite a chance. If Murray catches us, you flunk your solo."

"Owed you for taking the blame that first day of school." C.J. sneezed.

"Got an extra night of detention, big deal," I said. "This would've cost you an A."

"I know, but remember what you told me that day?"

"Not really."

Sirens wailed in the near distance.

"You told me, 'That's what pals do.' "

Before I could say anything more, Mrs. Murray hollered, "Phil, no talking. Get back in line."

Three fire trucks pulled up to the school's front entrance with sirens blaring and lights flashing. The firefighters rushed into the school.

Shortly afterward, Principal Knox gave the "all clear" signal. As we filed back into the building, I caught up with C.J. and good-naturedly slapped him on the back. "Thanks again," I told him, feeling the sheet music pinned under his sweatshirt.

"No problem," he said as we strolled into the band room.

By the time we took our seats, band was over. As I set my trumpet in its case, Mrs. Murray made her way to the podium and smacked her music stand with her baton.

"Everyone pipe down!"

The kids stopped chatting but continued packing up their instruments.

"One announcement before you leave. I hadn't counted on a fire drill, so I no longer have time to finish the solos before the semester ends. The test is canceled."

Almost all the band members hooted, hollered and whistled.

After we quieted down, Lana Woodfin, who liked to put up her hand to hear to her name called, raised her hand.

"Yes, Lana."

"Mrs. Murray, but what about kids who already tested?" Lana asked in her annoying squeaky voice.

"For those who tested, here's what I'll do. If the solo helped your grade, I'll count it. Otherwise,

I'll toss it."

The class cheered.

"You're dismissed. Enjoy the rest of your day."

"Gotta stop in the office," C.J. told me on the way out of the room. "Store my trumpet for me?"

"No problem," I said.

He handed me his trumpet case. "Thanks. See you in art," he said and took off for the office.

I stored our trumpets in my band locker and casually walked to art with a smile spread across my face. What a day. On the verge of butchering a piece of music I hadn't even practiced, a fire alarm saved me from embarrassment and a poor grade. Good old lucky number fourteen.

But the luckiest thing of all? Having C.J. as a friend. He risked his A to help me out and taught me a valuable lesson: never forget your friends.

RULE SEVEN

NEVER YELL AT A KID NAMED MOOSE

The collision sent my bag lunch—and me—flying down the hallway.

"Watch where you're going," I hollered to the jumbo-size bald boy as I raced to retrieve my lunch before someone mashed it.

The boy stopped dead and whirled around. It was Noah Fleming, but everyone called him Moose because of his size and brute strength.

"What'd ya say, tough guy?" Moose's voice sounded like a foghorn.

"You tell him, Moose," a pencil-thin boy yelled

from across the hallway.

Moose was much taller than me, outweighed me by a ton and looked meaner than a rabid racoon. He was no one to mess with.

"Whaddya starin' at?" A sneer formed on his lips.

"Nothing." I scooped up my lunch bag, relieved that nobody had stepped on my cucumber and liverwurst sandwich.

"Better not be, if you know what's good for you," Moose shouted as he plodded away.

Four sixth-grade girls leaving the library witnessed our exchange and laughed.

I didn't find anything funny about angering a bald, oversize oaf wearing eye black and a grass-stained muscle shirt.

A friend who owed me five bucks walked past Moose.

"Hey, Kirk," I yelled, hoping he had my money.

Suddenly, Moose whipped around and dropped his books on the floor. A flash of anger crossed his face. "Nobody calls me a jerk."

Moose arched his back and flexed his huge biceps. He let out a bloodcurdling scream before taking off like a cheetah after a gazelle. I couldn't believe a guy that big could move that fast.

I stood cemented to the floor, paralyzed by fright, as the human forklift barreled toward me bellowing at the top of his lungs. "You're … fish … bait!"

Fueled by fear, I beat a hasty retreat. A clean getaway was impossible, though, since hundreds of sixth graders were making their way to lunch. But as I weaved my way through the clogged hallway, Moose's battle cry stopped, and I slowed down and caught my breath.

Whew.

Figuring he'd lost interest in me and was on to other things, I took a quick peek over my shoulder to make sure.

But there he was, tearing down the hallway like a bruising fullback charging through a hole. Either kids leaped out of his way or he bowled them over with a fierce hip check as he flew by.

I kicked it into overdrive and ran for my life.

As I zigged and zagged through the mass of kids, I searched for help. Not a teacher in sight. *Where are they?* They always patrolled the hallways at lunchtime watching us, but now that I needed them, they were nowhere to be found.

As I darted into a narrow corridor, a skinny, long-legged girl suddenly rose in front of me. I tried to sidestep the beanpole, but my foot caught her leg causing us both to stumble. Before I could regain my balance, Moose hurdled the girl and tackled me. No player on the Frogs football team ever made a more sensational play. I lay there sprawled, my face mashed against the floor.

No match for Moose's lightning reflexes, he flipped me onto my back. Straddling my chest, he pinned my arms to the floor with his knees and jammed his giant forearm into my windpipe.

Other sixth graders stopped and gawked at me as if I were roadkill. One guy took out his phone and started recording.

"Didja call me a jerk, pipsqueak?" Moose said.

I gasped for air, and he removed his forearm. I sucked in three deep breaths. "I was yelling at my friend Kirk," I whimpered, my lips quivering.

Moose popped me on the forehead. "Liar."

I gulped in a lungful of air. "Honest, I was."

"Sure you were." Moose licked his chops. "Gonna be fun punching your lights out." He stuck his meaty fist in my face.

I was seconds from a beating I didn't deserve. Worse, the pounding would soon be posted all over the Internet. My only option was to apologize for something I didn't do. "S-s-sorry," I stammered.

Moose cracked his knuckles. "Say it like you mean it."

"Sorry," I squeaked out.

Moose leaned over and flashed me a nasty chip-toothed smile. Zits sprinkled his face like buckshot fired from a shotgun, and above his mouth was a hint of a mustache. He moved closer until we were nostril-to-nostril. His shirt reeked of cigarette smoke, and his breath smelled like a six-month-old taco.

I almost gagged.

"Last chance. Say you're sorry real loud before you lose your teeth." Moose balled up his right fist and cocked his arm, ready to strike.

Seeing his clenched fist took me back to the time Moose beat me up at a park when I was eight.

"Say it," he yelled.

"Sorry. Sorry," I screamed, picturing myself wearing dentures. My earsplitting apology echoed down the hallway, bouncing off the metal lockers.

The double apology worked. Moose got off me. But before letting me escape, he added to my shame. Bending down, he grabbed a fistful of my Milwaukee Brewers T-shirt with his grubby paw and yanked me close.

"What a dweeb," he announced to the crowd

while giving me a noogie sandwich. The hallway shook with laughter.

A moment later, a guy whispered loud enough for everyone to hear, "Fowler's coming up the stairs."

While the crowd scattered and Moose scrammed, I picked myself up off the floor and fled to the nearest bathroom. At the sink, I wiped off the beads of sweat that had formed on my face. I turned on the cold water, cupped my hands under the faucet and took a drink. As I shut off the water, C.J. came in with my lunch.

"You okay, Phil?"

"Yeah." I brushed off my jeans.

He lobbed me the brown paper bag.

I flashed him a grateful smile. "Thanks." I peeked inside to check its contents. My sandwich, graham crackers and juice box were still intact.

"Are ya brain-dead or do you enjoy getting beat up?"

"Meaning what?"

"You don't go around calling Moose a jerk."

"I didn't! I was yelling at Kirk."

The toilet flushed in the far stall, and then someone undid the latch. The door swung open and Shane stepped out.

"Whaddaya doing here?" I asked.

“Whaddya mean, what am I doing here?” he said in his you’ve-got-to-be-kidding-me voice. “I was dunking my dirty glasses in the toilet.”

I must’ve looked pretty foolish as Shane took off his black-rimmed glasses and held them out for me to inspect.

“See how clean they are? Boy, Phil, sometimes you’re as dumb as a shoestring.”

“Didn’t mean it that way,” I said. “And why aren’tcha wearing contacts?”

“Lost one.” Shane wiped the lenses with his shirt and put his specs back on.

“You look better with glasses, especially the way they’re bent in the middle.”

“Har har, Phil.” Shane adjusted the glasses on the bridge of his nose. “And why in the world would you yell at Moose? He’s tough, he’s mean and he’s wacko.”

“For sure,” C.J. chimed in. “He’s a biker dude in a kid’s body. No one messes with him, not even eighth graders.”

“I didn’t yell at him,” I said. “You think I’m crazy?”

“I heard he joined the Lost Creek Hoodies, the most feared gang in sixth grade,” Shane said as he walked to the sink.

“Heard that, too,” C.J. said. “You know, Phil,

to become a full-fledged Hoodie, you have to shave your head and harass a wuss."

"I guess you're the wuss," Shane said, washing his hands.

They both chuckled.

"You guys are a riot," I said. "Let's go to lunch."

In the cafeteria I nibbled on my liverwurst sandwich that was leftover from yesterday's dinner. The bread was dry and the meat tasted like kitty litter. Classmates stared and pointed at me, but I was surprised so few teased me. Relieved when the bell rang announcing the end of lunch, I took off for band.

For the rest of the day, concentrating was impossible. My mind kept drifting back to my close encounter with wearing dentures.

That night, while lying in bed, I reflected on my hair-raising run-in with Moose. Realizing I had come within a whisker of mimicking a crash test dummy, I made up my mind I was going to change. For the rest of the school year, I would never put myself in harm's way over a classmate's dumb remark or challenge a kid to a fight. And for sure, I would never yell at a kid named Moose.

RULE EIGHT

NEVER WEAR LOBSTER BOXER SHORTS TO SCHOOL

Ever want to crawl under a rock and stay there forever?

My troubles began early in the morning. After hopping out of the shower, I wrapped a towel around my waist, hustled into my room and pulled open my underwear drawer. “Mom,” I shouted downstairs, “where are all my boxers?”

“In the laundry room,” she yelled back. “The washing machine is broken. The repair guy won’t be here until noon. You’ll have to wear what’s there.”

I stared at the two pairs of boxers in the drawer

and shook my head. I examined the frayed gray pair and found the waistband badly torn, so I chucked them in the wastebasket.

The second pair was Grandma's Christmas gift—decorated with dozens of red lobsters swimming on a blue background—and they'd never been out of my drawer. Mom kept insisting I wear them so she could tell Grandma about it, but I'd been putting it off for two months.

Having no other choice, I shuddered and slipped them on. I hoped this made Grandma happy because I sure wasn't. This was going to be a one-and-done, and nobody would be the wiser. I finished dressing, ate breakfast and set out for school.

The morning went smoothly, and things got even better at lunch—Wednesday was pizza day. After going through the hot-lunch line, I sat with Shane and C.J. at our usual table.

"Are we playing volleyball in PE today?" Shane asked as I took a big bite of my slice of bacon-and-pepperoni pizza.

"Yup," C.J. said. "Our last day. Gymnastics start next week." He crammed a handful of cheese puffs into his mouth and licked his fingers.

I swallowed hard. "How can we play volleyball today when we had PE yesterday?"

"We have PE on odd-numbered days, right, Phil?" C.J. said and wiped off a glob of cheese stuck to his chin.

"Yeah, I know."

"Well, yesterday was February 29 and today is March 1. We have two odd days in a row."

My jaw dropped and my eyes flew open. I'd forgotten about leap year. If the guys saw my boxers in gym, I'd be toast.

"You okay, man?" Shane asked. "You're white as a marshmallow."

"Yeah. Just remembered I didn't shut off the shower."

No longer hungry, I set my half-eaten slice of pizza on my tray. While C.J. and Shane devoured the rest of their lunch, I mulled over ways to skip PE. Maybe I could catch the flu. Maybe I could sprain my wrist. Maybe I could hide in the bathroom. I needed to think of *something*. When the bell chimed signaling the end of lunch, I'd come up with zilch.

"Catch you guys in PE," Shane said after we dropped off our trays at the cafeteria window. He stuffed the rest of a Twix into his mouth and took off for French.

C.J. and I made our way to Spanish. Señora Ortega usually made Spanish fun, and today she began class by reviewing the language's grammar rules. I hung in there through Rule 4. As she discussed Rule 5—verbs and their tenses—I concluded that watching paint dry was more fun than listening to this.

Instead, I spent the rest of class trying to come up with an excuse to skip PE while observing "Josh the Miner" pick his nose and flick the boogers underneath his desk. Twenty minutes and countless boogers later, I still hadn't come up with an excuse for cutting gym.

I turned to Plan B. But for my plan to work, I had to cut out of Spanish early. With six minutes left in class and everyone working on the assignment, I strolled up to the teacher's desk. "Señora Ortega—"

She held her hand up like a crossing guard. "Just a minute, Phil. I have to write this note to myself before I forget."

As I waited, three thick books stacked on the far edge of her desk caught my eye. The top one was called *Spanish Grammar for the Utterly Confused*. The title summed up my relationship with the Spanish language perfectly.

When she finished, Señora Ortega set her pen on her desk. "Now, what can I do for you, Phil?"

"Can I return an overdue library book?"

She brushed her hair away from her face. "You know my rule, Phil. No one leaves class until the bell."

"But this is important, Señora Ortega. I promised the librarian I'd bring back the book right after lunch."

"You'll have to drop off the book after class."

"But Señora Ortega, I have—"

She raised her right eyebrow. "Phil, don't push it. Please sit down."

I returned to my seat, gathered my books and chewed my nails, waiting for class to end. For once I was grateful my last name began with *A*. Since Señora Ortega assigned seats alphabetically, I sat in the first desk in the first row, next to the door.

When the bell rang. I exploded out of my desk, burst from the room and tore down the hallway.

"Walk," shouted a teacher standing outside his classroom door.

I slowed down, but when he wasn't in sight anymore, I sprinted toward the locker room.

When I got there, the seventh graders were still filtering out, so I slipped through the side entrance. The room reeked of BenGay, BO and sweaty gym clothes. I hurried to my locker and undid my combination lock. I checked the room to make sure

I was alone before changing into my gym clothes in record time.

I heaved a sigh of relief. Since PE was my last class and nobody showered, I could stall, change into my street clothes after everyone left and still catch the bus. No one would ever know I had lobster boxers on.

I was sitting on a wooden bench in a washed-out Lost Creek T-shirt and black gym shorts when Shane and C.J. bounded into the locker room.

"What took you guys?" I joked.

"The way you split from Spanish, I thought your hair was on fire," C.J. said. "What's the rush?"

"Had to pee."

"Must've had to go bad." C.J. opened his locker.

"Almost wet my pants."

As my friends changed for class, Shane let loose a fart that sounded like air escaping from a party balloon. He snickered when he had everyone's attention.

"Call that a fart?" C.J. said.

"You can do better?" Shane said.

"No sweat, man." C.J. inhaled deeply, contracted his muscles and let one fly. The fart purred like a finely tuned motorcycle. "Not bad, huh?" he said.

"Top this, guys." I hunched over, squeezed my lips and let one rip. On a scale of one to ten on the Fart-o-Meter, the explosion registered a sixty-two.

The sonic boom rattled the lockers and lifted Shane and C.J. off the bench, almost knocking them onto the floor. Moving at the speed of smell, the stink bomb stunk up the room in nanoseconds.

"Give us a break, Abrams," a guy belted out as everyone fled for the exit.

"Boys, quit the horseplay and head to the gym," Mr. Mohr hollered from his office doorway, a police whistle hanging around his neck. "And who tried to blow out my office window?"

"Stinky Pants," C.J. squawked as he rushed past Mr. Mohr.

"Who's Stinky Pants?" Mr. Mohr asked.

"Abrams," C.J. told him.

"The smell almost did me in, Mr. Mohr," Shane said as he teetered past him.

Smiling, Mr. Mohr shook his head. "Feeling better now, Mr. Thunderpants?" he said as I passed his office.

"Never better, Mr. Mohr. Thanks for asking."

"Next time, Phil, use the bathroom. I can't have kids blowing craters in my lockers."

I chuckled. I loved Mr. Mohr's warped sense of humor. "The health teacher told us bottled up gas is dangerous," I said.

"Well, that answers that question." A smile crept over the gym teacher's face as if he'd solved a troubling mystery.

"What question, Mr. Mohr?"

"Why Mr. Fry always sits by himself in the teachers' lounge." Mr. Mohr had *that* look—the one adults have when they think something is funny but they know they can't laugh.

I pulled open the door, stepped into the gym and froze.

In the gym's far corner, a swaying rope hung from the ceiling. Rope climbing was part of the PE curriculum for boys. To demonstrate our upper-body strength, we had to climb the rope and ring a bell fastened to the ceiling while a teacher timed us. We kept trying until we passed. An eighth grader held the school record, ringing the bell in forty-one seconds. *He must be Spider-Man's cousin.*

For me, a scrawny sixth grader with spindle-like arms and rooster-like legs, ringing that bell had become a daunting task. The first time I tried, I climbed seven feet. But by doing countless push-ups and pull-ups in gym, I improved my upper-body strength. Each month, I climbed farther, but eventually I reached a plateau, falling four feet short on my last two tries.

When Mr. Mohr walked into the gym, he whistled everyone over. The class bunched around him for instructions.

"Everyone is on the same volleyball team and on the same court as yesterday," he said.

"What about me, Mr. Mohr?" Tara Washburn waved her hand. "I was absent."

Mr. Mohr ran his fingers down the clipboard he was holding. "Tara, you're on Team 8. Your court is next to the exit doors."

He paused and studied the clipboard. "One more thing. You boys who haven't passed rope climbing—Abrams, Madson, Owens, Yates—will join their teams after they try their luck on the rope. The rest of you report to your assigned court."

While the other kids dispersed to play volleyball, the four of us whose names were called met Mr. Mohr at the climbing rope.

"We'll go alphabetical, so you're up, Phil," the PE teacher said. "Let's ring the bell today." He dug into his baggy well-worn sweatpants and pulled out a stopwatch.

"I'll give it my best, Mr. Mohr," I said without much confidence.

Using both hands, I reached high on the thick rope, grasped it firmly and

hoisted myself up. I wrapped my feet around the rope and began climbing hand over hand. Inch by inch, I worked my way toward the bell.

"Keep going, Phil," Riley Yates hollered. "You're almost there."

I peeked at the bell. It hung three feet away. A personal best, but I was sapped and my arms ached.

"Come on, Phil, you can do it," Mr. Mohr said.

His encouraging words inspired me to keep going, and I inched up two more feet.

"You're too close to quit now," Mr. Mohr urged.

I glanced up. The bell hung a foot away. My arms felt like mush, but I climbed the last twelve inches. With one hand tightly grasping the rope, I reached out with the other and rang the bell.

Seven months of failure ended with that "ding." A mile-wide smile swept across my face.

"Way to go, Phil," Mr. Mohr shouted.

The guys waiting their turn to climb the rope applauded, and I looked down at them.

My smile vanished.

I'd never looked down from this high before and my heart was beating hard and fast. At that moment, I discovered that heights terrified me.

I glanced at the shiny bell and staring back in the reflection were panic-stricken eyes. Immobile, I clung to the rope like a life preserver.

"Madson, you're next," Mr. Mohr said.

"I can't go until Abrams comes down."

Mr. Mohr peered up at me. "Okay, Phil, shimmy down."

"I can't." I was too petrified to move.

"Why the blazes not? Glued to the rope?"

I didn't want anyone to know heights scared me, and Mr. Mohr's comment gave me an idea. I spit out my lame excuse. "I'm stuck."

"Impossible. Quit messing around and get down here."

"Stinky Pants is stuck in the rafters," a guy waiting in line hollered.

The other kids cut their volleyball matches short and moseyed over to watch me make a fool of myself.

While my classmates stared at me, Moose, who had a way of getting others riled up, pointed at me. "A dope on a rope," he shouted.

The gym rocked with laughter.

I was about to yell, "Shut up, you jerk," when memories of my encounter with Moose in the hallway came flooding back. The last thing I needed was another near beating.

"Knock it off, Moose," Mr. Mohr barked before looking back up at me. "Phil, your last warning."

To avoid further humiliation, I mustered my

courage and started down. As I readjusted my feet, though, my legs slipped off the rope and the drawstring holding up my gym shorts came undone. My shorts fell to my knees—exposing Grandma's Christmas present for the entire world to see.

While classmates ogled my boxers, my lobsters eyeballed them right back. I heard giggling, which then turned into laughter and finally into a full-throated roar that must've been heard a block away.

"Didja catch the lobsters yourself?" Moose yelled after the deafening laughter died out.

"Enough, Moose," Mr. Mohr said in a stern voice. "Phil, shimmy down."

Shamefaced, I inched my way toward the floor. Halfway, my arms felt as if they were being ripped from their sockets, and I loosened my grip on the rope. Big mistake. I skidded down, the coarse rope burning my thighs and my palms. *Thunk.* I hit the landing mat, feet first, twisting my left ankle. I toppled over, my face breaking my fall.

A searing pain shot through my leg, danced up my back and did somersaults in my brain. I lay on the mat in a crumpled heap, my left hand clutching the rope and my gym shorts halfway down my butt.

The crowd standing around the mat clapped, hollered and whistled.

"You can let go of the rope now, Abrams,"

Moose said, his voice dripping with sarcasm. "Your footsies are on the ground."

Everyone found Moose's wisecrack hilarious.

"Quiet!" Mr. Mohr ordered. "Next time, Moose, it's detention."

A hush fell over the spectators. Lightheaded, I scraped myself off the mat, hiked up my shorts and tied the drawstring tight.

"You all right, Phil?" Mr. Mohr asked.

"I'm fine," I said despite the throbbing in my ankle, too ashamed to say anything else. "Mr. Mohr, can I go to the locker room?"

"Abram's gotta change his panties," Moose announced to the crowd, which responded with hoots and howls.

"Everybody, knock if off," Mr. Mohr snapped. "Moose, see me after class."

The gym fell silent.

Mr. Mohr put his hand on my shoulder. "Take a break, Phil. Everyone else, back to your volleyball matches. Madson, you're up."

Eager to escape, I limped toward the exit on my gimpy ankle, wincing with each step. My ankle throbbed, and my palms and thighs burned, but nothing hurt more than my pride.

In the locker room, I hobbled to the drinking fountain and ran water on my palms. Then I wet a bunch of paper towels and gently dabbed my thighs to relieve the sting. After a long drink, I gingerly made my way to a bench and sat down.

I glanced at the clock hanging in the oversize office window. Twenty-nine minutes remained in class. If I went back into the gym, the teasing would be relentless.

I decided to skip the rest of PE.

After I changed into my street clothes, I noticed that the door of Moose's locker, down the aisle from mine, was ajar. I shuffled to Moose's locker, pulled out his jeans and limped to the drinking fountain, where I splashed water on the crotch. When it was saturated, I returned the jeans to his locker and sneaked out the side door.

Hoping no one asked me for my hall pass, I hobbled to the library and slumped onto an overstuffed beanbag. After examining my swollen ankle, I closed my eyes and waited for the dismissal bell. Despite my discomfort, I felt a faint smile of satisfaction cross my face.

The next day on my way to lunch, Mr. Mohr stopped me in the middle of the hallway.

Great, he's gonna bawl me out for skipping class.

"How are your palms and thighs, Phil?"

What? Why is he being so nice? "Uh, both still

hurt, but they feel better than yesterday."

"How's your ankle? The way you hit the mat, you're lucky you didn't break it."

We moved to the side of the hallway to avoid the onslaught of kids rushing to lunch.

"Swollen. I iced it with a bag of frozen berries when I got home. That helped."

"Good to hear," Mr. Mohr said. "I suppose kids hassled you about your boxers?"

"All morning." I leaned against the wall to ease the pressure on my ankle.

"Tell you what, Phil. Why don't you skip PE until next week and instead go to the library. By Monday your ankle should be fine. See me tomorrow before class and I'll write you an excuse."

"Thanks, Mr. Mohr. I can use the study time."

As I turned to leave, he said, "By the way, Phil, did you fool with Moose's jeans?"

"No, why?"

"Someone splashed water on them," Mr. Mohr said. "Looked like he wet his pants." He stooped down and picked up a felt-tip pen off the floor. He tightened the cap and slid the pen into his pants pocket.

"What a shame." I tried to hold back a smile.

I got the feeling from Mr. Mohr's half grin that he knew I'd done it.

He checked the hall clock. “Lunch duty calls. See you tomorrow.”

“Okay, Mr. Mohr.”

I limped into the cafeteria thinking that Mr. Mohr was a good guy. As I headed to the back of the long lunch line, the aroma of greasy hamburgers and french fries drifted through the air. My stomach growled. I forgot about Mr. Mohr and Moose. Stuffing myself was the only thing on my mind.

When I got home from school that day, I searched my bedroom hamper and retrieved Grandma’s Christmas gift. I balled the boxers up tight and buried them, lobsters and all, in the bottom of the trash so I’d never have to wear them again.

RULE NINE

NEVER GET IN THE WAY OF A PUKING CLASSMATE

Our target was Sara Winston, a pushy, stuck-up brown-noser cheerleader.

Everything about Winston begged for her to be put in her place. Her nose was always in the air, and she didn't just believe she was better than everyone—she was *sure* of it. My friends and I called her "SerWah," mostly because of how whiny she was, but also because she hated it.

SerWah's mission in life was to make Shane and me feel worthless. A week earlier, she'd made fun of our English project. Shane and I had spent Saturday morning working on a descriptive word collage for extra credit. In the center of a sheet of construction paper, we'd glued a picture of a cocker spaniel. Around the dog we pasted adjectives cut out from newspaper headlines, like *caring, playful* and *furry*. Before class SerWah noticed our collage pasted on the classroom wall.

"Hey, Abrams," she shouted, "don't you and Olson know *bravely* and *faithfully* are adverbs?" She put her hands on her hips as if she were posing before a camera. "How dumb are you guys?"

I sneered at her. "Not as dumb as you *look*, Ser*Wah*."

"If brains were rain, you two would be deserts," she broadcast to the class.

Our classmates laughed like crazy.

As I sank into my desk, I glared at her, and she turned up her button-like nose at me. I wanted to rip it from her stuck-up face and stuff it into her designer jeans. Before I could fire off a snappy comeback, Ms. Joyner came into the room.

"Everyone settle down," she said. "Take out your textbook and notebook."

As I grabbed my English book, I peered over my shoulder. SerWah sat at her desk with a smug expression on her face. I gave her the evil eye.

After taking attendance, Ms. Joyner strode up to

the lectern. "Today's lesson is using pronouns the right way."

I turned my head slightly and cupped my hand over my mouth. "Can't wait," I whispered to the girl sitting behind me.

She leaned forward in her desk. "Me neither," she said as if telling me a secret.

Forty-five boring minutes later, I dragged myself out of English and met Shane by the drinking fountain. "Boy, I hate Winston."

"Me, too," Shane said, "but what can we do?"

After I took a drink, I grinned. "Don't we dissect worms next week?"

"Yeah, why?"

"Let's give SerWah a worm sandwich."

"Aren't the worms toxic?"

"Nope," I said. "Mr. Jolly said the worms are chemical-free."

"That's right, he did," Shane said with a devilish smile.

At lunch, Shane and I hatched a plan to get back at SerWah. While we ate our spaghetti and meatballs, we agreed that my job would be to bring a plastic baggie from home and stash the worms in SerWah's sandwich. And so that we arrived in the cafeteria before it filled with students, Shane was to leave science early, ditch our books in his locker and get our bag lunches. We'd meet outside the teachers' bathroom near the cafeteria.

Next week couldn't come fast enough.

The following Tuesday, Mr. Jolly's science class dissected earthworms. Instead of throwing our worms away, Shane and I packed what was left of our experiments into a small zip-lock bag. I stuffed the baggie into my pants pocket.

As students cleaned up their workstations, Shane showed Mr. Jolly a fake note saying he had a doctor's appointment.

"See you in a few minutes," Shane told me as he plucked my books from the table and took off through the lab's rear door.

"Gotcha," I said. "Don't forget my lunch."

After class I zoomed out of the lab and met Shane in front of the teachers' bathroom.

"Thanks," I said when he tossed me my lunch bag. "Now let's motor."

Shane and I rushed to the cafeteria, where we stopped in our tracks. We stared in disbelief at the long rectangular table in the far corner.

"Where is she?" I said. "She's always the first one there." The jocks' table sat empty except for Matt Zahn, SerWah's boyfriend and the star guard on our sixth-grade basketball team.

“What a day for her to be late,” Shane moaned, “and what is Zahn doing here? He’s *never* early.” Shane threw his hands up in frustration. “Whadda we do now?”

“No idea,” I said, raising my voice. “We’ll never get another chance like this.”

Zahn got up and headed toward the vending machines at the lunchroom’s far end. He left a slice of pie and a sandwich lying on the table.

I turned to Shane. “Let’s hit Zahn instead.”

“Have you lost your mind? If he finds out, he’ll kick our butts.”

“He won’t find out if you stand guard and warn me if anyone comes.”

“I don’t know. He never did anything to us.”

“He’s SerWah’s boyfriend,” I said. “That’s good enough for me. Besides, the jocks think they run the school.”

“If we’re caught, Zahn will hate us forever.” Shane fidgeted with his belt buckle.

“He already hates us,” I said. “Did you forget last week in PE when he called us losers?”

“It’s too risky.” Shane glanced around uneasily.

“C’mon, don’t be such a wimp. Nothing’s gonna happen.”

“Oh, all right.” He shook his head like this was a bad idea. “But we gotta hurry.”

We panned the cafeteria to make sure no one was watching. Most kids were still making their way to lunch, and the dozen classmates already standing in the lunch line paid no attention to us. I handed Shane my lunch bag.

Shane scanned the cafeteria one more time. "The coast is clear. Make it fast."

I pulled on the rubber gloves I'd borrowed from the science lab. "Keep a lookout and holler if someone comes."

"Gotcha," Shane said, wringing his hands.

I scooted up to Zahn's table. With my heart racing, I pulled apart his ham and cheese sandwich and laid the bread slice on the table. I took the bag of worms from my pants pocket, unzipped the baggie and dumped the contents next to the sandwich. While setting the worms on the ham, one squirted through my fingers, bounced off the table and fell onto the floor.

"Hurry, Phil, before someone sees us," Shane said in a shaky voice.

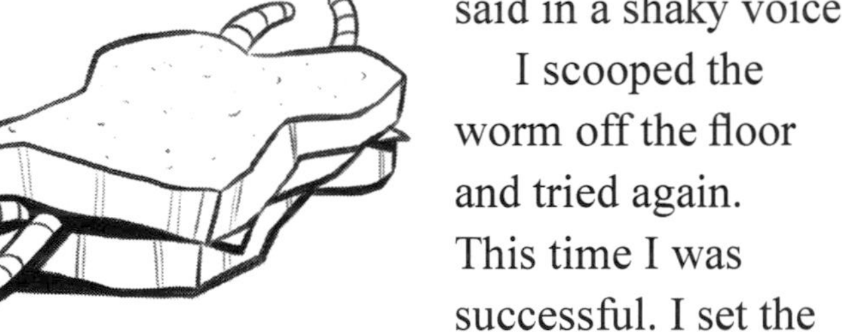

I scooped the worm off the floor and tried again. This time I was successful. I set the slice of bread on top of the worms, wiped the table with one of Zahn's napkins and beat it out of there. I ripped off the gloves and dumped them, the baggie and the napkin in a nearby trash barrel.

"I ditched the evidence," I told Shane as he gave me my lunch bag. "Now, let's find a table."

Not wishing to arouse suspicion but wanting a clear view of Zahn, we found a spot two tables from our target and took a seat.

Seconds later, SerWah paraded into the cafeteria. She strutted to the jocks' table like a peacock in full display, her long ponytail bouncing behind her. She sat down as if the spot were reserved for her. Making herself comfortable, she idly twirled her auburn ponytail around her finger and waited for her boyfriend and the rest of the basketball team to join her.

"That was close." Shane sounded relieved.

"Piece of cake," I said.

"Yeah, right. Then why are your hands shaking?"

I glanced down at my fingers. "Okay, maybe I was a little nervous."

By the time C.J. joined us, my hands had stopped trembling. "Why we sitting here?" he asked. "This isn't our usual table." He'd been at the dentist when Shane and I devised our plan.

"Thought we'd change things up," I said, not wanting to tell him the truth. "It's boring there."

I pulled a peanut butter and pickle sandwich, a six-pack of Oreos and a juice box from my lunch bag and set them in front of me. While shoving an Oreo into my mouth, I peered at the jocks' table.

Zahn sat next to SerWah as if they were glued at the hips. Four basketball players and SerWah's best friend, Lynne Whyte, filled the remaining seats. Because a game was scheduled for after school, the boys sported dress shirts and the girls were decked out in their cheerleading uniforms.

"What's this?" Zahn asked SerWah after seeing she'd taken a bite of his cherry pie.

She flashed him her phony smile and nestled her head against his shoulder. "The pie looked yummy." She playfully stuck out her tongue at her boyfriend.

"I'll fix you." Zahn snatched half of SerWah's sandwich, tilted his head back and opened his mouth as wide as an alligator's. He jammed the sandwich into the vast cavity.

"Hey. That's my lunch." SerWah grabbed Zahn's sandwich and took a huge bite. She chomped down, chewed heartily and swallowed.

A revolting look swept across her face. "This tastes disgusting." She pulled the sandwich apart and her eyes widened as she stared at the bread slices on the table. "What's *in* this thing?"

"Beats me," a basketball player said.

"No clue," a teammate chimed in. "Whatever it is, it's gross."

"It's cut-up worms," the lanky center said, genuinely surprised. He bit into his egg-salad sandwich.

"How do you know that, smarty-pants?" one of the players asked.

The center swallowed. "'Cuz—" He cleared his throat. "'Cuz we dissected worms in science today."

"Worm guts." The expression on Zahn's face was priceless. "You guys put worm guts in my sandwich."

"Don't blame us. We had nothing to do with it," the center said. Like a bunch of bobbleheads, the other players nodded.

SerWah began to speak, but before she could utter a word she let out a loud belch.

A sickened look filled her face. Covering her mouth, she scrambled from her seat, but she was too late. She didn't just puke—she erupted like a volcano. Puke ran down the front of her orange V-neck sweater and black skirt. What missed her outfit splattered on the table, and what missed the table sprayed onto the floor.

Lynne and the players jumped to their feet and backed away from SerWah like she was radioactive.

"Lost my appetite," the center said and dropped his half-eaten sandwich into his brown paper bag.

"Me, too," Lynne said, tossing the rest of her cupcake into the garbage.

SerWah squealed. Her high-pitched cry pierced the crowded, noisy lunchroom. Everyone stopped eating and peered in the direction of the jocks' table.

Delighted at the unexpected turn of events, I felt a smile stretch across my face. I stuffed another Oreo into my mouth.

"Who screamed?" C.J. asked. Along with Shane and three hundred other sixth graders, he rose to his feet to see what the fuss was all about. "Something happened at the jocks' table."

"Zahn probably spilled his milk," I said. "The jocks have to make everything a big deal."

"SerWah puked on herself," C.J. said in amazement. "You gotta see her, Phil."

"No kidding." I stood to see, but scads of curious sixth graders had gathered near the jocks' table. Even stretched up high on my tiptoes, I could barely see SerWah, so I snaked my way through the throng to get a good view.

As it turned out, seeing SerWah drenched in puke was better than acing an English test. I wanted to run up to her, pump my fists high in the air and holler, "Is *pukey* an adverb?" at the top of my lungs.

The crowd applauded as SerWah rose from her chair. Half-digested food fell onto her spotless white sneakers or landed on the floor. Her skirt dripped a liquid that could have passed for tomato juice.

"Smells like a septic tank," a guy yelled.

Some kids clamped their hands over the mouths and noses or pinched their nostrils. Three or four gagged, struggling to hold down their own just-eaten lunches.

"Hope everyone is enjoying this," the humiliated cheerleader cried out while sidestepping the foot-wide puke puddle on the floor.

"We are," a spectator hollered.

I grinned.

SerWah ran a tissue over her mouth and checked out her sweater and skirt. The more she inspected her outfit, the angrier she became. Trying to help, Zahn handed her a napkin, but when she looked at it, she threw a hissy fit that would have made a three-year-old proud.

"What am I supposed to do with one napkin?" she shrieked. "Some boyfriend you are."

"That's the only napkin I had," Zahn said, looking startled. "What else do you want me to do?"

"Buy me a new outfit," SerWah wailed. "After all, the sandwich was *yours*." Wiping her hands with the napkin and tossing it onto the table, she turned and faced the crowd. Her eyes were wild as they darted around at everyone staring at her.

Searching for a way out, she headed straight in my direction. The sickening smell must've gotten to her because, when she got to me, she puked on my Packers sneakers.

The crowd exploded with wild laughter.

I stood there aghast. "SerWah," I yelled. "What the …"

With tears streaming down her cheeks, SerWah made her way through the backpedaling crowd. She ran down the hallway in the direction of the locker rooms, leaving a puke trail behind her.

With my classmates' laughter ringing in my ears, I hustled toward the locker rooms, too. Once there, I peeled off my sneakers and threw my socks into the trash. Carrying my shoes by the laces, I went into the bathroom and removed the plastic bag lining the wastebasket. I stuffed my sneakers inside the bag and tightly knotted it shut. I set it on top of a row of lockers, figuring no one would dare steal it.

Shane found me washing my hands. "Incredible. First SerWah, then you."

"Glad you enjoyed the show." I turned off the faucet and dried my hands. "Hope my sneakers aren't ruined."

"Yeah, SerWah did a number on them."

"I'll try cleaning them when I get home. But for now, what am I gonna wear for PE?"

"I got a pair of old high-top sneakers in my gym locker, but no socks."

"Thanks," I said. "Don't need socks. Have an extra pair in my locker."

"You've gotta admit, Phil, that was great. And even though SerWah wrecked your sneakers, we got her back."

"Keep it down," I said in a low voice. "Someone might be in the locker room. We tell no one, not even C.J."

Shane lowered his voice, too. "Got it."

Once we were dressed for PE, we sat on a bench and waited a few minutes before our classmates arrived.

"Man, was SerWah puking on herself cool or what?" C.J. said, spinning his locker combination. "And boy, Phil, did SerWah get you."

"Ha ha. By the way, did you find out what happened?" I asked, playing dumb, something my sister had told me I'd mastered.

"Someone stashed worm guts in Zahn's sandwich," he said as he started changing. "SerWah swallowed a bite of his sandwich and puked."

"Awesome," I said. "Serves her right."

"For sure," Shane added. "SerWah craves the spotlight. The drama queen got her wish."

"I hope Zahn doesn't find the dude who pulled

this stunt," C.J. said. "If he does, the guy is in for a serious butt-kicking."

"How do you know it's a guy?" I said.

"I don't." C.J. put his foot on the bench and started tying his sneaker. "I'm assuming it's one of his basketball buddies, but whoever did this is a brave soul."

"I'll say." Shane glanced my way.

As C.J. locked his locker, he said, "You must have a sixth sense, Phil."

"Why do ya say that?" I asked.

"We move to a different table because you said nothing ever happens at our old spot. Ten minutes later the lunchroom is in an uproar."

"Lucky, I guess." I stood to leave.

"And another thing. The kid who pranked Zahn must have Jolly for science."

"How do ya figure?"

"'Cause Jolly's classes are the only ones dissecting worms this month."

I gulped.

Shane and I exchanged quick worried glances. Instead of three hundred sixth-graders who could have carried out the prank, there were actually only a hundred on the list. I pulled an imaginary zipper across my lips to make sure Shane kept silent. He nodded.

I nibbled on my fingernails as I walked out of the locker room and into the gym.

✓ ✓ ✓

That evening at home, Mom came into the kitchen as I was about to set my vomit-encrusted sneakers in the dishwasher. She wrinkled her nose.

"Phil, what are you doing and what's that awful smell?"

"Cleaning my sneakers. A girl puked on them at lunch."

"You'll do no such thing."

"But, Mom, these are my Packers sneakers."

"Set them in the laundry room next to the washing machine. I'll try to salvage them, but don't count on it."

I slipped my sneakers into a new trash bag, twist-tied it shut and carried it to the laundry room.

That night in my dreams, I replayed the entire wacky, up-and-down day. Thanks to our clever planning and a little luck, the prank had started well. SerWah ended up eating the worms, puking and having a world-class meltdown. As an added bonus, Zahn blamed his teammates for the practical joke.

But like my day, my dream turned into a nightmare. In the wrong spot at the wrong time, I stood stunned as SerWah puked on my shoes. Worse, everyone assumed she'd gotten me. And to top it off,

I'd most likely seen the last of my Packers sneakers.

My nightmare ended with SerWah mocking me in a whiny voice, with a hint of barf on her breath: "Got ya again."

I woke up soaked in sweat, switched on the lamp and jumped out of bed. After grabbing a handkerchief off my dresser, I dried my face and wiped my hands on my pajamas. I found a red pen on my desk and got out my Rules of Never notebook. At the top of the ninth page, I scribbled Rule 9: "NEVER GET IN THE WAY OF A PUKING CLASSMATE."

Back in bed, I couldn't get the image of SerWah barfing on my Packers sneakers out of my mind. Needless to say, I didn't sleep much.

RULE TEN

NEVER LIKE SOMEONE WHO CAN BREAK YOUR HEART

Clara Starling taught me five lessons in a single day.

Clara had moved into the school district in March and became an instant hit with the boys, me included. Goose bumps ran down my arms the first time she strode past my desk in math. The scent of freshly picked raspberries trailed her down the aisle.

Clara had no problem getting boys to notice her. Her cute dimples and sparkling eyes melted a boy's insides. Her golden hair with a reddish streak running through it hung a third of the way down her back. She always wore blush, fingernail glitter and lip gloss, but never too much. Cheerful and outgoing, her dazzling smile rivaled a supermodel's.

Too afraid to talk to her, I'd only dreamed of meeting her until fate brought us together. One morning in the hallway, Clara dropped her pencil case, and both of us stooped to pick it up. When our heads collided, she giggled for some strange reason.

"Sorry, so sorry," she said between giggles. The way she said "sorry" let me know she meant it, but banging heads was no big deal.

I stood awestruck, my heart thumping like a jackhammer. I gazed blankly at her, and her vivid blue eyes stared back. I wanted to say something witty, but it seemed as if a gigantic hairball were stuck in my throat. My lips moved but nothing came out.

Clara tilted her head to one side and waved her hand in front of my eyes. "*Hello*. Earth to Mars."

I snapped out of my trance.

"Totally my fault." Clara ran her fingers through her hair and flashed me her megawatt smile.

My fingers tingled, my knees turned to jelly and my mouth dried up. More nervous than a chicken in a fox's den, I sputtered, "Th—that's okay." Tongue-tied, I did the first thing that entered my mind: I felt my noggin for a lump.

"I'm Clara." She stuck out her hand. "You all right? You seem a bit woozy."

Flustered, I swallowed the golf ball-size lump in my throat. "My name is … Fine … and yeah, I'm Phil." I shook her hand but for far too long.

"You can let go now, Fine." She chuckled good-naturedly. "Are you headed to math?"

I took a deep breath and let it out slowly. "Yeah," I managed to say.

"Mind if I tag along?"

"Not at all," I said, surprised at my good fortune.

Though I found it hard to talk to her, she seemed happy to keep the conversation going. During our short walk to math, I found out she enjoyed snowboarding, playing softball and cheesy black and white horror movies.

When we got to the classroom, I leaned against the doorframe and watched Clara glide down the aisle. After she slid into her desk, she tucked three strands of hair behind one ear and winked at me.

I stood spellbound.

"Phil, please take your seat," Mr. Fowler said.

"Sure, Mr. Fowler." I floated to my desk.

I wanted to turn around and stare at her during class, but I had enough problems in math. I forced myself to pay attention, knowing she sat only four desks behind me.

After class, C.J. and Shane stopped me in the hallway.

"I see you got the hots for Clara," C.J. said.

"Whaddya mean?"

"You looked like a space cadet standing in the doorway."

"Yeah, right."

"Forget her, Phil. You got no chance," Shane said. "Girls like Clara don't dig guys like us."

"I can dream, can't I?"

As the days passed, Clara's and my "hellos" became more frequent and our chats lasted longer. I found her easier to talk to, and we spent more and more time together at school.

One day after math, she surprised me. "Phil, do you want to go together?"

"Not sure," I answered, not knowing what "going together" meant.

"Let's go together," Clara said. "You don't have to give me a ring or anything." She squeezed my hand. "It just means we like each other best."

Since I already liked Clara best, I quickly agreed. "Sounds great."

As I made my way to science my heart swelled. I realized that, for the first time in my life, I had a girlfriend.

The next three weeks zipped by, with Clara and

I passing each other sappy notes and trading warm glances in math, the only class we shared. I printed her name in black marker on my sneakers. She scribbled my name on her notebook covers. We swapped

email addresses, texted each other and talked on the phone. I visited Clara at her locker before school and hung out with her after lunch, even though C.J. and Shane teased me about it.

I walked her home from school a few times, and twice we did math homework together at her kitchen table. A math whiz, she finished every problem ahead of me.

As I pedaled home after the second math session, I mulled over how my life had changed since I met Clara. My grades were better, and I hadn't been grounded in a month. To top it off, I was going with the prettiest and one of the smartest girls in sixth grade. C.J. and Shane even stopped teasing me. My world was perfect.

Three days later, as I unlocked my locker to get my books for my morning classes, Clara approached me. "Phil, can I talk to you for a sec?"

"Sure," I said. "What's up? Can't meet me after lunch?"

She pressed her lips together for a long moment and then blurted out, "I don't think we should see each other anymore."

Thunderstruck, I stood frozen for what seemed like forever. "Why not?" I finally asked. A knot formed in the pit of my stomach.

"My parents feel we're getting too serious."

"Too serious? Do they think I'm gonna marry you or something?"

"No, nothing like that."

The knot tightened. I sensed by her expression that this wasn't about her parents. "What gives?"

As Clara fingered her necklace, she looked me right in the eye. "The truth is, I like someone else."

My insides twisted into a million pretzels and my jaw dropped. "W—wh—when did this happen?" I stammered, raising my voice several decibels.

"Over the weekend. I've liked him for a while, but he was going with Sara Winston until two weeks ago. They had a big fight in the lunchroom and broke up."

"*What*? You like *Matt Zahn*?" I slumped against my locker.

"I'm sorry." Clara pushed her hair back over her shoulders, pivoted on her heels and walked away.

My heart sank to my toes as she strode down the hallway, her hair swaying from side to side. She quickly disappeared around a corner. I'd flunked tests, broken my leg and flooded a school bathroom, but Clara's breaking up with me was by far the lowest point of my life.

And once she'd mentioned Zahn, I knew I had no chance of winning her back. To girls, Zahn was a dreamboat. But I had a different opinion—I considered him a "too." He was too smart, too athletic, too cool and too popular. He got any girl he wanted.

I pulled my books out of my locker and slammed the door, and as it closed, its jagged edge snagged my T-shirt. The shirt became wedged between the door and the frame, pinning me against my locker.

I dropped my armload of books on the floor and pulled up the locker's handle, but the door was jammed tight. I stood helpless, my cheek pressed against the cold metal locker, as classmates filed by on their way to class. All gawked and most giggled, but no one offered to help.

C.J. finally wandered by. "Phil, if you're kissing your locker, do it when nobody's around. You look like a dork."

"Shut up and get me unstuck."

When he pried open the door, a torn paperback, a

fast-food wrapper, a crushed soda can and an empty potato chip bag fell out. C.J. peered inside.

"Dumpsters have less trash than this," he said, picking the junk up off the floor.

"Everyone can't be a neatnik like you," I said.

"It's called being organized." He crammed the bag and wrapper inside the paperback and lobbed the book and the can back into the locker.

"Yeah, but you're off the charts. Who else lines up pencils on his desk by length or has boxers arranged in his drawer by color?"

"So I like stuff in order. So what? By the way, your locker needs an air freshener. Smells like sewer gas."

"Speaking of things that stink, Clara dumped me."

"When?"

"Just now."

"Bummer, man." C.J. sneezed into his elbow. "Clara's supercool."

"Tell me something I don't know." With my spirit broken like a ridden wild mustang, I scooped up my books, closed my locker and trudged to English with a hole in my heart. But nouns and pronouns were the last thing on my mind.

By the time I stepped into Mr. Jolly's fourth-period

science class, I'd calmed down.

Mr. Jolly was a cool guy, but his room looked a lot like my locker. Wall-to-wall clutter lay on the back counter. A small aquarium with a cracked side sat on one end. On the other end stood an old popcorn machine coated with grime.

Among the litter in between were a collection of unidentified rocks, a cardboard box of broken beakers, old lab experiments and an out-of-date "Phases of the Moon" calendar. Two geraniums in serious need of water hid the Laboratory Safety Chart.

Of all the stuff strewn around, the one item that interested most of us was a dusty stuffed raccoon named Bandit that snoozed on a shelf above the back counter. A hairy spider we called Rhonda had spun a web between Bandit's ears. Judging by the web's size, Rhonda had lived there for awhile.

"We have lab today," Mr. Jolly announced after taking roll. "The experiment is called 'saltwater egg.' If done correctly, you will learn the concept of density. The handout at your workstation will explain the procedure you're to follow."

Mr. Jolly's labs were loads of fun. We always discovered something new, and kids bustled around and talked freely. If I was going to get my mind off Clara, lab was the place.

Our goal was to find out if an egg floated in tap water or in salt water. My partner was Nicole Gabinski. Teachers called Nicole "gifted" and loved having her for a student. I loved having a brainiac for my partner—with her help, I aced every lab.

While Nicole pored over the coffee-stained handout, I noticed Zahn perched on a stool in front of the room. Clara's new boyfriend acted as if he didn't have a care in the world. The more I watched him, the angrier I became.

As Nicole filled two tall plastic cups with tap water, I pocketed a straw from a storage bin. I ripped off a pea-size piece of paper from my lab notebook and rolled the paper into a tiny ball.

I slipped the ball into my mouth and worked it until the paper was soaked. I stuck the straw between my lips and loaded it with the spitball. While Nicole dumped tablespoons of salt into one of the cups, I aimed the straw at the back of Zahn's head. Just as I fired, Nicole bumped my elbow.

Oh, no.

The spitball whizzed past Zahn's arm, skimmed off a table and onto Mr. Jolly's desk. The slimeball kept rolling until it bounced off his pinkie.

Rummaging through a drawer hunting for something, Mr. Jolly suddenly looked up. Shielding his eyes from the bright ceiling lights with both hands, he scoured the room.

I ducked behind Nicole but was too late. Since I was still clutching the straw in my hand, Mr. Jolly homed in on me.

"Phil, what are you doing?" He eyed me with suspicion.

Classmates quit working on their experiments and focused their attention on me. Nicole unzipped her pencil case and took out her inhaler. Was she worried the excitement might cause her to start wheezing?

I dropped the straw between the two water-filled cups. "Seeing if eggs float in saltwater, Mr. Jolly."

"Really? Because I thought you were shooting spitballs in my lab." He had a grim expression on his face.

I'd crossed the line and had no easy way out.

Mr. Jolly straightened his polka-dot bow tie, pushed himself from his seat and marched my way. Obviously struggling to control his temper, he clamped his teeth down on his lower lip. Any harder and he'd have bitten a hole right through it.

"I'd never … do such a thing, Mr. Jolly," I said, fumbling for words and trying to appear innocent. My pulse quickened. Marble-size beads of sweat trickled down my forehead and dropped onto the table, creating a tiny shallow pond.

Mr. Jolly, whose rumpled pants and wrinkled short-sleeve shirt looked like they'd been slept in, stopped at our table. "Then explain, young man, why a straw is lying on your workstation?"

"In case I get thirsty," I said, trying to worm my way out of a bad situation.

My classmates chuckled.

Mr. Jolly stood stone-faced with his hairy arms folded across his chest. "Fork over the straw, Phil."

Busted, I handed him the straw, which he bent in half and stuffed into his pants pocket.

"Report to my room at 3:10." He wagged his index finger at me. "Don't be a second late."

As Mr. Jolly walked away, I noticed he'd tucked his dress shirt into his boxers, which stuck out above his waistline. I laughed but muffled the sound by nervously mopping my face with my "Save the Whales" T-shirt. I hoped Mr. Jolly hadn't heard me. I was already in a boatload of trouble.

Nicole put her inhaler away and the rest of lab passed quietly.

After the last bell, I reported back to the lab. Mr. Jolly quit tinkering with a stapler and checked his watch.

"Right on time, Phil," he said in a gruff voice. He motioned to a stool in the front row. "Take a seat."

I set my backpack and my hoodie on the table behind me, pulled out a stool and sat down.

"Now, where is that straw?" Mr. Jolly asked himself, scratching his chin.

I waited as he rummaged through his desk for the confiscated straw. While digging through a third drawer, it dawned on him that the straw was in his pants pocket. He handed me the straw, placed a pile of scrap paper on my table and parked a wastebasket six feet in front me.

"After you shoot thirty spitballs into the basket, you may leave. Kids tell me you're an expert marksman, so this shouldn't take you long." Mr. Jolly sauntered back to his desk and hunkered down in his chair to read a well-worn copy of *How to Organize Your Science Lab*.

Although the wastebasket was a short distance away, the crimp in the straw decreased my accuracy. For each spitball I made, I missed two or three. After missing three straight shots, I glanced at the ancient clock radio on Mr. Jolly's desk: 4:12.

"Mr. Jolly, can I text my mother and tell her I'll be late for dinner?"

"Fine. The way you're missing the basket, you may be late for breakfast." He smiled, but it wasn't a happy smile or an angry smile. It was more of a self-satisfied smile, as if he was getting revenge for all the wrongs ever committed in his classroom.

And he wasn't far off. I'd only made sixteen shots in an hour. At this rate, I'd be here past five. I dug my phone out of my backpack and texted Mom.

"at school helping mr jolly. will b late 4 dinner."

"ur father will b upset," she texted back.

Not wanting to get into a lengthy exchange about my father's view on family gatherings, I punched in, "cant b helped" and sent the text on its way. I shut off the phone and stashed it in my backpack. I was glad I had ridden my bike to school. Walking home would take forever.

Fifty-four minutes later, I hit basket Number 30. It took another three minutes to pick up all my air balls before Mr. Jolly would let me leave. With my mouth feeling like a huge canker sore, I walked out to my bike, knowing that my parents wouldn't believe I'd helped Mr. Jolly for two hours. As I hopped onto my bike, the solution occurred to me: I'd deflate my front tire a block from home.

And that's what I did. I half-ran that last block dragging my Schwinn behind me. I wheeled the bike into the garage, leaned it against the back wall and strolled into the house.

Starving, I stepped into the kitchen scrounging for leftovers. My father sat at the table sipping coffee and reading the sports page of the local newspaper. Mom was clearing the table, and Kaylee was loading the dirty plates and used silverware into the dishwasher.

"What was for dinner, Mom?" I said with my head in the fridge.

"Texas chili. On the second shelf."

Uh-uh. Never again on a school night. Instead, I grabbed three slices of day-old pizza and a jug of chocolate milk.

As I closed the fridge, Dad paused between sips of coffee. "It's 5:33. Mr. Jolly kept you this long?"

It sounded much more like an accusation than a question. I stalled, pretending I hadn't heard him.

"I'm waiting for an answer, son." No doubt about it—Dad was in one of his no-nonsense moods.

"Kinda." Lame, but I couldn't come up with anything else.

"Explain 'kinda,' Phil." Dad folded the newspaper in half, set it on the table and poured himself another mug of coffee.

"I left school in time for dinner," I said, "but my bike had a flat. Some jerk let the air outta my tire."

"So that's why you walked your bike into the

garage," Mom said as she cleaned the stovetop.

"Yeah. And—"

"Oh, my gosh, Phil. What happened to your lips?" Mom asked.

"What do you mean, Mom?"

"They're swollen."

"Probably tried kissing Rhonda and she bit him," Kaylee said.

"Funny, Kaylee. That's the last time I tell you anything." I rubbed my index finger across my lips. They felt puffy. I shot Kaylee an angry look. She glowered back, her eyes squinting and her lips curled upward. She knew she'd stuck it to me.

"Who's Rhonda?" Mom asked.

"A spider living in the science lab," Kaylee explained.

"Oh," Mom said with a confused look on her face.

"Camels have smaller lips than yours," Dad said, pouring cream into his coffee. "You didn't get into a fight at school and have to stay after, did you?"

"No, Dad."

He swirled his coffee with his fork. "Then what's with the lips?"

Stumped for a reasonable explanation, heartsick over my breakup and peeved about having to stay after school, I confessed.

I told my parents that Clara had dumped me. I

explained that when I saw her new boyfriend having fun in science lab, I got mad and shot a spitball at him. And I told them how Mr. Jolly had punished me, but I skipped the part about deflating my tire.

When I was done explaining, Mom had a pained look on her face. On the other hand, my father remained calm, as usual. He took a sip of coffee and set his mug on the table.

"Phil, I understand why you were upset, but what were you thinking? What if you had hit someone in the eye?"

"Dad, everyone wears safety goggles in lab."

"Doesn't matter," Dad said in a stern voice. "You're confined to your room Saturday for shooting spitballs and Sunday for lying. No TV. No iPod. No PlayStation. No phone. No laptop."

"C'mon, Dad. Haven't I been punished enough? I was just paying a guy back for—"

He cut me short with a wave of his hand. "I've made up my mind, and that's the end of it."

To avoid making matters worse, I didn't push the issue. Besides, arguing with my father was pointless. Once he made up his mind, he never changed it. No longer hungry, I put the pizza and milk back in the fridge and stomped from the kitchen.

"If I catch you using anything off limits, you'll be grounded for a month," Dad called after me.

I stormed upstairs, pushed open the door to my room and kicked the door shut behind me.

That weekend, I did homework, reread my Batman comic book collection, gawked at a blank TV screen and watched two spiders race back and forth across the ceiling. The hours passed like days. By Sunday I was so bored that I cleaned my room. I also had time to realize five important things before hitting the sack that night.

The first was that actions, including spur-of-the-moment ones, have consequences.

Second, lying to my parents was a lousy idea. Being grounded was bad enough, but worse was the hurt in my mother's eyes when she discovered I'd been lying. I never wanted to see that look again.

Third, being banished to my room for a weekend with nothing to do was no fun.

The fourth was the toughest and most painful. Liking someone could break your heart. I was positive I'd never recover.

Finally, I learned that it wasn't smart to write a girl's name on my sneakers in permanent marker. Since they were my last pair, I had to wear them to school, and I knew that every time I did, I'd think of Clara.

By the way, I also added shooting spitballs to my Rules of Never list.

RULE ELEVEN

NEVER FAIL TO PREPARE

I set my books on my desk and plopped into my seat. Ms. Joyner took roll as the PA crackled to life. "Good morning, students and staff," Principal Knox said. "Here are today's announcements:

- Today's quote is from Ben Franklin: 'By failing to prepare, you are preparing to fail.'
- Hot lunch today is mac and cheese, a cup of yogurt, milk and a raisin cookie.
- Friday is class color day.

- ✦ The boys' and girls' track teams have a meet at Franklin at 4:15.

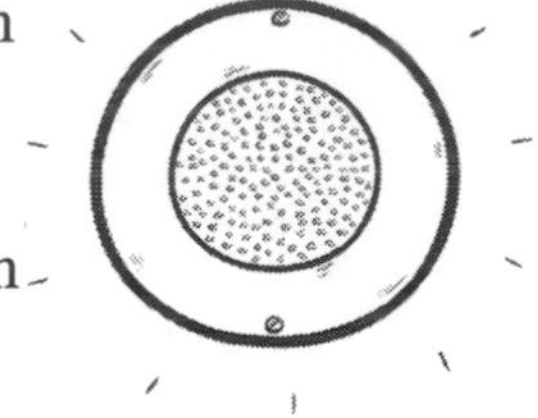

- ✦ Next year's Battle of the Books list can be picked up in the library.
- ✦ Tickets for Saturday's dance can be purchased for fifty cents at the bookstore.
- ✦ Phil Abrams and Shane Olson are to report to the office immediately after announcements.
- ✦ Have a terrific Wednesday."

"Terrific for everyone but me," I muttered.

I felt a gentle tug on the back of my T-shirt. "What did you guys do now?" Ellen Anderson asked in a low voice so Ms. Joyner wouldn't hear.

I twisted my head slightly and whispered, "We laughed when the librarian tripped over a stack of books."

"Let me guess. The librarian didn't find it funny." Ellen snickered.

I nodded.

"Phil and Shane, you may leave for the office," Ms. Joyner said. I picked up my books and met Shane in the hallway.

"Didn't go to detention either?" I said.

"Nope. Had something to do after school."

"Like what?"

"You'll see," Shane said with a mysterious smile. "Why didn't you go?"

"Forgot."

We dumped our books in Shane's locker and took off to meet our fate.

A short time later, Shane and I walked into the office and ambled up to the counter. "We're here to see Mr. Mullen," I told the secretary.

"Have a seat." She gestured to a pair of white plastic chairs next to the large office window and picked up the phone. "Two boys are here to see you."

We waited a few minutes before Mr. Mullen stepped into the outer office. "Glad you weren't too busy to decline my invitation," he said in a booming voice that brought back some not-so-fond memories. "Follow me."

He led us into his office. "Sit," he ordered as he took a seat behind his desk.

I sat down and checked out the room. Nothing had changed since my visit on the first day of school. The office had the same dull gray walls, the same pictures and the same misspelled nameplate. The only difference was the potted cactus sitting on top of the black file cabinet was now dead. Mr. Mullen had probably scared it to death.

The assistant principal tapped a pencil on his desk calendar. The way his eyes bored into us was creeping me out. He set the pencil down. "Know why you're sitting here, boys?"

I squirmed in my seat. "I guess it's because we missed detention."

"You guessed right, Abrams."

His phone rang but he ignored it. "I'm busy so I will make this quick." He eyed me intently and I rubbed my sweaty palms on my pant legs. "Since this is your second visit to my office, Abrams, I'm tripling your detention. You will stay after school tonight, Thursday and Friday. Got it?"

Rather than cooking up some story and getting caught lying, I played it safe and said, "Yes, sir."

Mr. Mullen printed my name and the dates on a detention slip and handed it to me.

He then directed his attention to Shane. "This is your first offense, Olson, so you'll stay after school tonight and tomorrow. Understood?"

"But I have an excuse," Shane said.

"You do?" Mr. Mullen rested his arms on his desk. "Can't wait till you share it with me."

Shane took a deep breath. "It's my mom's fault."

"Your … mom's … fault?" Mr. Mullen's eyes widened behind his round-rimmed glasses. "Exactly how does she fit into this?"

I was curious myself. I sat up straight, tilted my head toward Shane and got ready for his explanation.

"She needed me to babysit," Shane said with a quiver in his voice. "If I had stayed after school, my little brother would've been home alone."

"Let me get this straight." Mr. Mullen settled back in his chair and locked his fingers behind his head. "You're blaming missing detention on your mother."

Shane swallowed hard. "That's right."

Mr. Mullen ran his hand over his closely cropped hair. "Why didn't you inform me about this problem yesterday?"

"Didn't know I had to."

Mr. Mullen's eyes narrowed. "I went over every school rule at orientation."

"Wasn't there," Shane said. "I transferred in."

I clamped my hand over my mouth to smother a smile.

"Next time, tell me if you can't stay after." Mr. Mullen coughed hoarsely. "We can work something out."

"I will. Promise."

"Are you babysitting today?" Mr. Mullen coughed again.

"Today, tomorrow and the next day."

"*What?*" Mr. Mullen reared out of his chair, knocking over his full coffee cup with his elbow. His calendar and a clutter of papers got drenched, and a cascade of coffee ran down the side of his desk and pooled on the carpet.

I sat stunned and speechless, but by the time the empty paper cup rolled to a stop, I found myself struggling to stifle a full-blown laugh. I could tell Mr. Mullen was ticked by the way he was muttering under his breath. And the longer it took him to soak up the mess, the madder he got.

Half a roll of paper towels later, he finally plunked back down in his chair. "We'll see about that!" he barked at Shane and opened the top drawer of his desk. He pulled out a yellow legal-size pad and set it in front of him. The pad was the only dry item on his desk.

"How can I get hold of your mother, Olson?" he said, red-faced, and plucked a blue pen from his shirt pocket.

"You can call her at work." Shane told him his mother's cell number.

Mr. Mullen pulled his chair closer to his desk and jotted down the phone number on the pad of paper.

He shot Shane a testy look. "You'd better be telling the truth," he said in a sharp tone. "I don't take lying lightly."

"I am, Mr. Mullen."

Mr. Mullen punched in the number Shane had given him and rolled his chair away from us. After about thirty seconds of speaking too quietly for us to hear, he swung back to face us, rubbing his temple.

The assistant principal cleared his throat. "Your mother was displeased you skipped detention, but she backed up your story," he told Shane after hanging up the phone.

Shane let out a quiet sigh.

"Even though you have a legitimate excuse, Olson, I can't let you off scot-free." Mr. Mullen stuck the pad of paper back into his desk drawer. "You will report to isolated lunch today."

The phone rang. As he picked it up, he warned us not to get into trouble again and sent us on our way.

We hastily left the office and, once out of earshot, burst out laughing. "The coffee deal was awesome," Shane said. "That was worth a trip to the office."

"Yeah, that was amazing," I said as we dawdled to Shane's locker. "And so was the way you lucked out and had to babysit."

"Luck had nothing to do with it."

"Whaddya talking about?"

"Had this all planned."

We stopped in front of his locker. "What? You're kidding, right?"

"Nope. I knew I had detention, so I volunteered to babysit my brother after school."

"Genius," I said.

"I know." Shane smirked. "Isolated lunch is better than detention."

"For sure," I said as we grabbed our English materials from his locker.

"Remember the Ben Franklin quote from the morning announcements?"

"Something like, 'If you don't prepare, you fail.' So?"

"What old Ben said is more poetic than that. Anyway, it's easier to remember my version: 'Never fail to prepare.' "

"I wish you would've mentioned that before I tried the halfway con."

"I forgot."

"Thanks for nothing. I still get the chills every time it rains."

Shane laughed and closed his locker.

We headed off to English.

RULE TWELVE

NEVER SHOVE A BIG BUTT INTO A SMALL OPENING

I can best describe my last day of sixth grade in one word: bizarro.

The morning started out uneventfully. Since we only had a half day of school, we had an extended homeroom and four short classes. We cleaned out lockers, returned textbooks and heard a farewell speech from each teacher.

Fourth-period science had barely begun, when Principal Knox's voice burst over the intercom.

"Hope everyone is having a fantastic day. Two brief announcements. First, staff changes for next school year are as follows: Our head cook, Mrs. Hart, will be moving to Hamilton Elementary. Eighth-grade teachers Mrs. Taylor and Mr. Lewis will be retiring along with seventh-grade teacher Mrs. Jackson. Also, Ms. Joyner will no longer be teaching sixth grade."

Our class erupted with cheers.

"Instead, Ms. Joyner will join the seventh-grade faculty."

The cheers turned into moans and groans. Three boys seated in the far side of the room sobbed.

"Finally, the staff and I wish you an enjoyable and safe summer. Congratulations to our eighth graders, and we look forward to seeing the rest of you in September."

A short while later, as Mr. Jolly finished addressing our class, I sat impatiently at my desk waiting for the bell. In nine minutes and thirty-four seconds, I would be sitting on the school bus, beginning my long-awaited summer vacation.

The bell finally rang. Noisy and excited, my classmates and I raced to our homerooms because this was the first year that sixth graders would receive their own yearbook.

"I'm not handing out yearbooks until everyone sits down and stops talking," Ms. Joyner said, raising her voice.

We quickly found our seats and quieted down.

As she passed out the yearbooks, I eagerly opened mine. Since student pictures were arranged alphabetically, my photo would be easy to find.

I flipped to the second page and cringed.

The photographer had taken two headshots of me on the third day of school. One had been halfway decent, but in the other I looked like the biggest dork in sixth grade. The photographer had sent the publishing company the wrong picture.

I slumped down in my desk. This was far worse than when the world saw my lobster boxers or when Loose Lips caught me with my pants down. My classmates might forget those mishaps, but my yearbook photo would haunt me for all eternity. Every time they browsed through their yearbooks, they'd see my dorky picture.

As if reading my mind, SerWah jumped up from her desk and hollered, "Hey, Abrams." She held up her yearbook and pointed at my picture. "Do you need a license to look like that?"

Not wanting to draw attention to myself, I gave her a death-like stare but said nothing. As I checked the wall clock, the bell rang. I stuffed my yearbook into my backpack and dashed from the room. I made my way to the parking lot, boarded the bus and took a seat. It wasn't long before C.J. plopped down beside me. As I sat feeling sorry for myself, I heard a familiar voice from the back of the bus.

"Watch this!"

Before I'd even turned around, I knew who it was. Moose.

While the other riders and I watched, Moose unlatched a window facing the school and slid it open. He jumped up onto the torn seat, bent over and stuck his big fanny out the window.

All year, Moose had tormented teachers, stressed out office staff and bullied classmates. Now the Terror of Sixth Grade was giving Lost Creek a parting shot before leaving for summer vacation.

As the bus lurched forward, the outside supervisors stood frozen in place. Their mouths flopped open, and their double-wide eyes were glued to Moose's rear end. Kids standing single file to board their final bus ride home roared their approval as we rumbled from the parking lot.

Unlike the kids waiting in line, nobody on our bus cheered. Four boys knelt on their seats to get a better view. The other riders remained seated but kept their eyes fixed on the bully.

"Moose's a scuzzball," I whispered to C.J. "Hope he gets stuck."

I despised Moose not only for making fun of me in school but also for what he'd done to me at a park when I was in second grade. While two friends and I waited to take our turn on a slide, Fleming cut to the front of the line.

"Hey, Fleming, the line starts there." I pointed to the end of the line.

"Whatcha gonna do 'bout it, twerp?"

I kept as silent as an empty church.

"Too scared, huh?" Fleming said.

I peered at the ground.

"That's what I figured."

"You're up, Fleming," a guy in line yelled.

As the bully climbed the steps, I turned to my friends and said a little too loudly, "What a butthead."

Fleming wheeled around and sneered. "I heard that, Abrams." He backed down the slide and strutted up to me, shaking his fist. He jabbed my stomach with his pudgy finger, shoved me to the ground and kicked me in the ankle.

"Slides aren't for crybabies, Abrams," he said as I lay on the grass bawling. "You better go home to Mommy."

Not wanting to be humiliated in front of my friends, I stopped crying and scrambled angrily to my feet. Although he had more muscles in one arm than I had in my whole body, I didn't care. I balled my fingers into a fist, reared back and punched him in the mouth with all my might. Amazingly, his bottom lip split open like a ripe tomato, and blood poured down his chin.

"I'm gonna pound you good, Abrams," Fleming yelled, spitting blood everywhere. His eyes grew fierce as he dragged the back of his hand across his chin to wipe away the blood.

Then he hit me again and again—like bullies do. The beating ended when my friends jumped him. Outnumbered, Fleming fled like a spooked rabbit.

Now, as I sat on the bus, that day at the park ran through my mind. I hated Moose more than ever. He was showing everyone what he thought of Lost Creek. I wished I had the guts to show him my opinion of *him*.

"Fleming, park your butt in the bus," the driver, Ed Pierson, ordered in his gravelly voice. "You boys kneeling on the seats, sit down."

While he was watching the commotion in the mirror, he drove over two traffic cones as the bus exited the parking lot. "Everyone sit down! Now!"

The kids who were kneeling obeyed, but Moose ignored Ed's orders.

"If I have to stop this bus, Fleming, you'll walk home," Ed bellowed. The kids on Bus 353 knew the burly bus driver meant what he said.

"Yeah, yeah," Moose said. "Don't get your undies in a bundle."

But when Moose tried pulling his fanny inside the bus, he couldn't move.

"I'm stuck," he called out. "Somebody help me."

No one lifted a finger. I guess they felt like I did—they'd rather get a sharp stick in the eye than help the bully. I for one enjoyed watching Moose squirm and wiggle, trying to free himself like a rat caught in a trap.

Seeing Moose's plight, Ed pulled the bus to the curb. The bus groaned to a halt alongside the teachers' parking lot. He turned off the engine, activated the hazard lights and rose from his seat.

"Everyone stay seated," he barked as he stormed down the aisle. When he got to Moose, he grabbed him by the arms and tugged, but the lunkhead didn't budge. He tried a second time—still nothing.

Giving Moose an exasperated look, Ed tried one more time before giving up. The bus driver paused for a moment, a sly smile appearing on his face. He rubbed his hands together like he was going to enjoy what he was about to do.

"Ain't you gonna help me?" Moose shouted.

Ignoring Moose's plea, Ed trudged back to the front of the bus. When Ed reached his seat, he knelt and removed a large crowbar stored underneath it.

Moose's hands started to tremble. "You're not using that, are ya?"

"Don't worry," Ed said, sounding sincere. "It's not big enough."

Everyone howled with laughter.

"So funny I forgot to laugh," Moose said. "Now get me free."

"Aren'tcha glad I talked you into taking the bus?" C.J. asked me.

"Yeah," I said. "Wouldn't miss *this* for the world."

Ed set the crowbar on the floor, fetched a first-aid kit from under his seat and pulled two rubber gloves out of it. He hauled himself to his feet and faced us. With great flair, he pulled on the gloves and raised his hands above his head. "Dr. Ed will now perform fanny surgery."

Everyone cheered.

Ed opened the door, stepped off the bus and grabbed a footstool from a storage compartment. We leaped from our seats and jockeyed for the best view. We poked our heads out windows, knelt on seats or stood in the aisle on our tiptoes and craned our necks.

All eyes were glued on Ed as he stepped onto the stool and planted a hand on each butt cheek. He gave the bully a hearty shove, but Moose didn't move an inch.

"You're stuck good," Ed said after four futile tries. "I'll need help. Boys, pull Moose by the arms while I push."

"Not gonna hurt, is it?" Moose whined.

"Hope it hurts a ton," I half-whispered to C.J., who grinned.

"I doubt it," Ed told Moose, "but it's the only way I can free you." He moved the stool a foot closer to the bus. "Here goes, Fleming."

Moose clenched his jaw and squeezed his eyes shut.

"On three, boys." Ed stepped onto the stool again. "One, two, three."

On three, Ed pressed his right shoulder into Moose's dangling rear end while six boys yanked

Moose's beefy arms.

Finally, Moose flew into the bus, but his cargo shorts snagged on the window's edge.

R-r-i-i-p-p-p.

The bully lost his balance, crashed headfirst onto the seat and tumbled into the grimy aisle.

We all let out a thunderous cheer.

The big oaf struggled to his feet and examined himself. Except for his torn shorts, it appeared that he'd survived the ordeal intact. But then, nothing ever hurt him. His head was made of concrete.

But he *had* fallen into a sticky substance that looked like spilled soda. It covered the bottom of his tan shorts and the backs of his hairy legs.

Ed climbed aboard and stood at the front of the bus. "I warned you, Fleming, if I had to stop the bus, you'd hoof it home. So start walking."

"You can't do that," Moose yelled.

"Oh yes I can. Now get off my bus." He pointed to the door.

"Make me." Moose plunked himself down on the seat, folded his arms over his chest and glared at Ed.

Ed reached into his pants pocket and pulled out his phone. "Do I need to call Principal Knox?"

Moose shot Ed a dirty look. The bully snatched his backpack from the floor, stood and hoisted the backpack over his shoulder. He charged down the congested aisle toward the exit, pushing kids aside as he went.

"I'm gonna sue you and the bus company!" he screamed at Ed as he stomped off the bus.

Ed shrugged, slid his phone back into his pocket and looked at the rest of us with a goofy grin.

As he peeled off one of the gloves, he curled his nose as if a vile odor had seeped from the glove. Holding it shoulder high, he dropped it into a small trash bin beside his seat. Then he performed the same routine with the other glove.

We erupted in cheers.

"Dr. Ed at your service," he said, taking a bow.

We clapped louder.

"Now, kids, please sit." Ed waved his hands in a downward motion and plopped down in the driver's seat.

The ovation died down and we took our seats. Ed slapped the door shut, fired up the engine and put the bus in gear.

As I watched Moose hike home, all the rotten things he'd done to me flashed through my mind. Ignoring all common sense, I poked my head out the window and hollered, "Hey, Moose, enjoy walking home with all your friends."

Moose spun around and swaggered toward the

bus. Seeing the bus creep into traffic, he stopped and spit in my direction.

"Just so you know," I shouted, "I'm the guy who soaked your jeans in gym."

"You're toast, Abrams." He shook his fist at me. "Catch ya later."

"Can't wait," I yelled back as he stormed off.

"Have you lost your mind?" C.J. said. "The next time Moose sees you, he's gonna break your face."

"Won't be a next time," I said. "His house is for sale. He's moving to Indiana."

"You better hope he moves before school starts."

I hoped so too. If not, Moose, who held grudges for years, would make sure my first day in seventh grade began on a bad note.

By the time C.J. and I stepped off the bus, I was no longer worried about Moose or my dorky yearbook photo but looking forward to a fun summer.

"You know, Moose did us a favor," I said as we set off for home.

"How did he do that?"

"He taught us a valuable life lesson."

"What's that?"

"Never shove a big butt into a small opening."

We both cracked up.

EPILOGUE

A bunch of stuff happened in the last nine months—some good, some bad, some funny, some not so funny. Despite the rough patches, I survived my first year in middle school.

And as I was busy surviving, something happened to me. I changed. I came to see school and people differently.

Sixth grade forced me to either grow up or get left behind, to deal with situations I didn't understand or didn't want to understand. I learned a lot every day, not only about school but also about life. I went into sixth grade a kid and came out a teenager—well, almost a teenager.

Adults and classmates have asked me what I'll remember most about sixth grade. I'm sure I'll never forget Wide Track, Ms. Joyner, Moose or SerWah. I'll smile when I think of Clara—it only took me a month to get over her even though I thought I never would—and I'll cringe when I think of my lobster boxers and my yearbook picture. But as for my fondest memories, those are the times I spent with my friends C.J. and Shane.

And next school year? My parents told me it will be full of new adventures, new lessons and new challenges. When I asked them if I'll need a new Rules of Never, they just grinned.

Seventh grade, here I come.

ABOUT THE AUTHOR

After a distinguished 34-year career, Phil Adam retired as a middle school teacher from Ashwaubenon, Wisconsin. His ongoing passion for teaching and commitment to his profession, coupled with a unique ability to connect with students, earned him a Wisconsin Middle School Teacher of the Year designation.

Phil declines to comment on the extent to which *The Rules of Never* is based on his experience as a teacher . . . or as a student.